Alice eats

ALICE'S
ADVENTURES IN
WONDERLAND
by Lewis Carroll
with recipes inspired by
the story and characters

Alice eats

A WONDERLAND COOKBOOK

words and pictures by

PIERRE A. LAMIELLE

and

JULIE VAN ROSENDAAL

whitecap

Table of Contentments

"What is the use of a cookbook," thought Pierre, "without a story, drawings, photographs and recipes?" So he considered the idea of a cookbook based on the beloved storybook *Alice's Adventures in Wonderland*. It seemed a wonderful idea, so he asked his wonderfully talented and generous friend Julie over for crumpets.

They discussed the *Wonderland* idea over tea, and as they ate more crumpets and drank more tea, the idea grew and grew. With culinary references woven into all the facets of the storyline, and with food items appearing as obstacles that Alice must embrace or overcome throughout her journey in Wonderland, it made sense to create recipes to accompany the plot from beginning to end.

They started by making a list, chapter by chapter, of yummy Wonderland delicacies that would reveal themselves during Alice's adventure. And there was room to create a timeless Mad Hatter tea party.

After delving into the culinary side of the project, Pierre got to work on his illustrations. He has created a unique, colourful set of images that is unlike any previous incarnation of this iconic nineteenth-century tale.

Julie set to work crafting and testing recipes and taking photos along the way. She provides her gorgeous photography to enhance the aesthetic richness of the recipes and to provide many visual points of reference to help in the cooking process, making the volume both beautiful and practical.

Their hope is that this book is a sumptuous read for lovers of food and classic literature (and those who love to stash cookbooks on their bedside table), as well as an inspiration to kids, to get them into the kitchen and cook, create new dishes and host a mad tea party.

Alice Eats draws all of us—the Mad Hatters and the March Hares, the Cheshire Cats and the Queens of Hearts, the Caterpillars and the Alices—to the table, together, to toast our similarities and differences and everything else that makes this world such a crazy and delicious place in which to be. Pull up a chair, and we'll pour the tea.

—*Julie Van Rosendaal & Pierre A. Lamielle*

CHAPTER 1

Down the Rabbit-Hole

Alice was beginning to get very tired of sitting by her sister on the bank, and of having nothing to do: once or twice she had peeped into the book her sister was reading, but it had no pictures or conversations in it, "and what is the use of a book," thought Alice "without pictures or conversation?"

So she was considering, in her own mind (as well as she could, for the hot day made her feel very sleepy and stupid), whether the pleasure of making a daisy-chain would be worth the trouble of getting up and picking the daisies, when suddenly a White Rabbit with pink eyes ran close by her.

There was nothing so *very* remarkable in that; nor did Alice think it so *very* much out of the way to hear the Rabbit say to itself, "Oh dear! Oh dear! I shall be late!" (when she thought it over afterwards, it occurred to her that she ought to have wondered at this, but at the time it all seemed quite natural); but when the Rabbit actually *took a watch out of its waistcoat-pocket*, and looked at it, and then hurried on, Alice started to her feet, for it flashed across her mind that she had never before seen a rabbit with either a waistcoat-pocket, or a watch to take out of it, and burning with curiosity, she ran across the field after it, and was just in time to see it pop down a large rabbit-hole under the hedge.

In another moment down went Alice after it, never once considering how in the world she was to get out again.

The rabbit-hole went straight on like a tunnel for some way, and then dipped suddenly down, so suddenly that Alice had not a moment to think about stopping herself before she found herself falling down a very deep well.

Either the well was very deep, or she fell very slowly, for she had plenty of time as she went down to look about her, and to wonder what was going to happen next. First, she tried to look down and make out what she was coming to, but it was too dark to see anything: then she looked at the sides of the well, and noticed that they were filled with cupboards and book-shelves: here and there she saw maps and pictures hung upon pegs. She took down a jar from one of the shelves as she passed: it was labelled "ORANGE MARMALADE," but to her great disappointment it was empty: she did not like to drop the jar, for fear of killing somebody underneath, so managed to put it into one of the cupboards as she fell past it.

"Well!" thought Alice to herself, "after such a fall as this, I shall think nothing of tumbling down stairs! How brave they'll all think me at home! Why, I wouldn't say anything about it, even if I fell off the top of the house!" (which was very likely true.)

Down, down, down. Would the fall *never* come to an end!? "I wonder how many miles I've fallen by this time?" she said aloud. "I must be getting somewhere near the centre of the earth. Let me see: that would be four thousand miles down, I think—" (for, you see, Alice had learnt several things of this sort in her lessons in the schoolroom, and though this was not a *very* good opportunity for showing off her knowledge, as there was no one to listen to her, still it was good practice to say it over) "—yes, that's about the right distance—but then I wonder what Latitude or Longitude I've got to?" (Alice had not the slightest idea what Latitude was, or Longitude either, but she thought they were nice grand words to say.)

Presently she began again. "I wonder if I shall fall right *through* the earth! How funny it'll seem to come out among the people that walk with their heads downwards! The Antipathies, I think—" (she was rather glad there *was* no one listening, this time, as it didn't sound at all the right word) "—but I shall have to ask them what the name of the country is, you know. Please, Ma'am, is this New Zealand or Australia?" (and she tried to curtsey as she spoke—fancy *curtseying* as

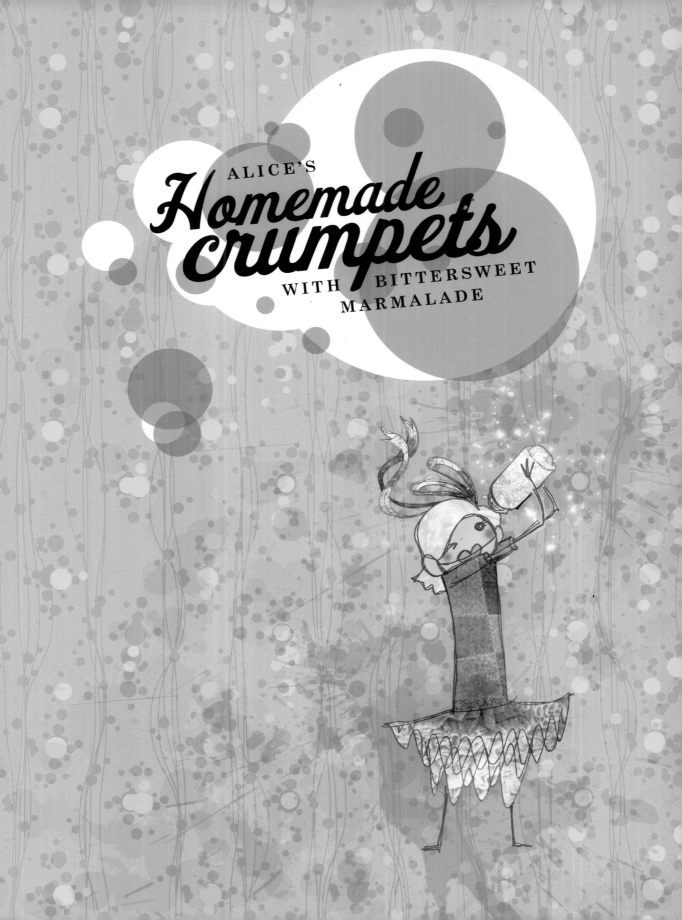

ALICE'S

Homemade crumpets

WITH BITTERSWEET
MARMALADE

Homemade Crumpets

Crumpets are riddled with holes. Sometimes those holes go on
for what seems like miles, which is perfect for filling with
lots of melty butter and Alice's Bittersweet Marmalade (see page 11).

Makes about 2 dozen crumpets, depending on the size of your rings

Ingredients

- 2 tsp (10 mL) or 1 pkg active dry yeast
- 1 tsp (5 mL) sugar
- 2¾ cups (685 mL) warm water, divided
- 3 cups (750 mL) all-purpose flour
- 1 tsp (5 mL) salt
- 1 tsp (5 mL) baking soda
- 2 Tbsp (30 mL) warm water
- canola oil, for cooking

Alice's advice

You'll need crumpet rings or round stainless steel cookie cutters to cook these on the stovetop, but the pleasure of freshly made crumpets means picking up a set is worthwhile.

In a large bowl, stir the yeast and sugar into 1 cup (250 mL) of warm water. Let sit for 5 to 10 minutes, until it starts to get foamy; if it does nothing, toss it out and buy fresh yeast.

Add the flour, salt and another 1¾ cups (435 mL) of warm water, and stir until you have a wet, sticky dough. Cover with a tea towel and set in a warm place for an hour or so, until the dough has risen slightly and is all bubbly on the surface.

In a small dish, stir the baking soda into the 2 Tbsp (30 mL) of warm water, and stir into the dough. Let it sit for another 20 minutes.

When you're ready to make crumpets, preheat a heavy skillet (cast iron works very well) with a drizzle of oil over medium-low heat, and spray the inside of a set of crumpet rings or round biscuit cutters with nonstick spray; run around the inside with your fingers to grease them evenly. (Alternatively, use the oil and your fingers or a paper towel to grease them on the inside.)

Place a few rings at a time in the skillet, without crowding (leave about ½-inch/1 cm between them), and fill each halfway with batter. Let cook for 7 to 8 minutes, until bubbles start to burst through the surface.

Flip the crumpet over, remove the ring and cook for a few more minutes, until golden on the other side and cooked through.

Set aside to cool on a wire rack while you make the rest of the crumpets. Serve warm.

Bittersweet Marmalade

Stash your marmalade in labelled jars in the cupboard so that when there are fresh warm crumpets to be eaten, you'll never be stuck with an empty jar. Then watch the marmalade dash quickly down the crumpet holes.

Makes about 4 cups

Ingredients

3 large oranges
5 cups (1.25 L) water
pinch salt
4 cups (1 L) sugar
1 vanilla bean (optional)

Alice's advice

Including the orange seeds during the cooking process will incorporate more pectin, which thickens the marmalade. Keeping the seeds in a tea ball or wrapped in cheesecloth will make it easy to remove them afterward.

Cut the oranges in half and poke the seeds out; put the seeds into a tea ball if you have one, otherwise wrap them in a small piece of cheesecloth, pinning the cloth to fasten it.

Slice the oranges thinly and then chop them crosswise as chunky or fine as you like.

Put the sliced oranges and the tea ball into a pot with the water and salt and bring to a boil; simmer for half an hour. Turn off the heat and let sit for a few hours.

Stir in the sugar and bring the mixture back to a boil. Simmer for about half an hour, or until the mixture gels. You can test it by dropping a small spoonful onto a saucer that has been chilled in the freezer while the marmalade simmers. Drop a spoonful onto it, and if you can drag your finger through and leave a trail, it's ready.

If you're using a vanilla bean, cut it lengthwise with the tip of a sharp knife and scrape out the seeds.

Remove the tea ball and stir the vanilla seeds into the marmalade. Divide the marmalade into clean, warm jars and tuck in the vanilla pods if you like. Seal according to the jar manufacturer's directions to store in the cupboard, or let cool completely and store in the fridge or freezer. Serve on toast or homemade crumpets.

you're falling through the air! Do you think you could manage it?) "And what an ignorant little girl she'll think me for asking! No, it'll never do to ask: perhaps I shall see it written up somewhere."

Down, down, down. There was nothing else to do, so Alice soon began talking again. "Dinah'll miss me very much to-night, I should think!" (Dinah was the cat.) "I hope they'll remember her saucer of milk at tea-time. Dinah, my dear! I wish you were down here with me! There are no mice in the air, I'm afraid, but you might catch a bat, and that's very like a mouse, you know. But do cats eat bats, I wonder?" And here Alice began to get rather sleepy, and went on saying to herself, in a dreamy sort of way, "Do cats eat bats? Do cats eat bats?" and sometimes, "Do bats eat cats?" for, you see, as she couldn't answer either question, it didn't much matter which way she put it. She felt that she was dozing off, and had just begun to dream that she was walking hand in hand with Dinah, and saying to her, very earnestly, "Now, Dinah, tell me the truth: did you ever eat a bat?" when suddenly, thump! thump! down she came upon a heap of sticks and dry leaves, and the fall was over.

Alice was not a bit hurt, and she jumped up on to her feet in a moment: she looked up, but it was all dark overhead: before her was another long passage, and the White Rabbit was still in sight, hurrying down it. There was not a moment to be lost: away went Alice like the wind, and was just in time to hear it say, as it turned a corner, "Oh my ears and whiskers, how late it's getting!" She was close behind it when she turned the corner, but the Rabbit was no longer to be seen: she found herself in a long, low hall, which was lit up by a row of lamps hanging from the roof.

There were doors all round the hall, but they were all locked; and when Alice had been all the way down one side and up the other, trying every door, she walked sadly down the middle, wondering how she was ever to get out again.

Suddenly she came upon a little three-legged table, all made of solid glass: there was nothing on it but a tiny golden key, and Alice's first thought was that this might belong to one of the doors of the hall; but, alas! either the locks were too large, or the key was too small, but at any rate it would not open any of them. However, on the second time round, she came upon a low curtain she had not noticed before, and behind it was a little door about fifteen inches high: she tried the little golden key in the lock, and to her great delight it fitted!

DINAH'S
Saucer of Panna Cotta
AT TEA TIME

Saucer of Panna Cotta

A saucer of milk is far easier for a cat like Dinah to lap up at tea time.
Little girls with good table manners prefer spoons for eating their cream,
and to have it infused with tea and sweetened with honey.

Makes 8 small saucers full

Ingredients

- 4 cups (1 L) half and half or 18% cream
- 1 Tbsp (15 mL) plain gelatin (1 pkg)
- ¼ cup (60 mL) honey
- ½ tsp (2 mL) vanilla
- 1 Tbsp (15 mL) good-quality loose tea leaves

Alice's advice

Use any kind of good-quality loose tea leaves to infuse flavour into your panna cotta—the tea you choose will determine the panna cotta's flavour.

Pour the cream into a medium pot and sprinkle the gelatin overtop. Let it sit for a few minutes to let the gelatin soften. Set the pot over medium heat and stir, warming the cream but not letting it boil, until the gelatin is completely dissolved.

Add the honey and cook, stirring, until melted and smooth. Remove from the heat and stir in the vanilla.

Add the loose tea leaves and let infuse for 3 minutes. Strain the tea out through a fine-meshed sieve. Discard the tea.

Pour the cream into small individual dishes or ramekins and refrigerate for at least 2 hours, until set. (This recipe can be made up to a few days in advance; cover each dish with plastic wrap to avoid having the cream dry out on top.)

Alice opened the door and found that it led into a small passage, not much larger than a rat-hole: she knelt down and looked along the passage into the loveliest garden you ever saw. How she longed to get out of that dark hall, and wander about among those beds of bright flowers and those cool fountains, but she could not even get her head through the doorway; "and even if my head *would* go through," thought poor Alice, "it would be of very little use without my shoulders. Oh, how I wish I could shut up like a telescope! I think I could, if I only knew how to begin." For, you see, so many out-of-the-way things had happened lately that Alice had begun to think that very few things were really impossible.

There seemed to be no use in waiting by the little door, so she went back to the table, half hoping she might find another key on it, or at any rate a book of rules for shutting people up like telescopes: this time she found a little bottle on it ("which certainly was not here before," said Alice), and tied round the neck of the bottle was a paper label, with the words "DRINK ME" beautifully printed on it in large letters.

It was all very well to say "Drink me," but the wise little Alice was not going to do *that* in a hurry. "No, I'll look first," she said, "and see whether it's marked '*poison*' or not": for she had read several nice little histories about children who had got burnt, and eaten up by wild beasts, and other unpleasant things, all because they *would* not remember the simple rules their friends had taught them: such as, that a red-hot poker will burn you if you hold it too long; and that, if you cut your finger *very* deeply with a knife, it usually bleeds; and she had never forgotten that, if you drink much from a bottle marked "poison," it is almost certain to disagree with you, sooner or later.

However, this bottle was *not* marked "poison," so Alice ventured to taste it, and, finding it very nice (it had, in fact, a sort of mixed flavour of cherry-tart, custard, pineapple, roast turkey, toffee, and hot buttered toast), she very soon finished it off.

"What a curious feeling!" said Alice, "I must be shutting up like a telescope!"

And so it was indeed: she was now only ten inches high, and her face brightened up at the thought that she was now the right size for going through the little door into that lovely garden. First, however, she waited for a few minutes to see if she was going to shrink any further: she felt a little nervous about this; "for it might end, you know," said Alice to herself, "in my going out altogether, like a candle. I wonder what I should be like then?" And she tried to fancy what the flame of a candle looks like after the candle is blown out, for she could not remember ever having seen such a thing.

After a while, finding that nothing more happened, she decided on going into the garden at once; but, alas for poor Alice! when she got to the door, she found she had forgotten the little golden key, and when she went back to the table for it, she found she could not possibly reach it: she could see it quite plainly through the glass, and she tried her best to climb up one of the legs of the table, but it was too slippery; and when she had tired herself out with trying, the poor little thing sat down and cried.

"Come, there's no use in crying like that!" said Alice to herself, rather sharply. "I advise you to leave off this minute!" She generally gave herself very good advice, (though she very seldom followed it), and sometimes she scolded herself so severely as to bring tears into her eyes; and once she remembered trying to box her own ears for

having cheated herself in a game of croquet she was playing against herself, for this curious child was very fond of pretending to be two people. "But it's no use now," thought poor Alice, "to pretend to be two people! Why, there's hardly enough of me left to make *one* respectable person!"

Soon her eye fell on a little glass box that was lying under the table: she opened it, and found in it a very small cake, on which the words "EAT ME" were beautifully marked in currants. "Well, I'll eat it," said Alice, "and if it makes me grow larger, I can reach the key; and if it makes me grow smaller, I can creep under the door: so either way I'll get into the garden, and I don't care which happens!"

She ate a little bit, and said anxiously to herself, "Which way? Which way?" holding her hand on the top of her head to feel which way it was growing; and she was quite surprised to find that she remained the same size. To be sure, this is what generally happens when one eats cake; but Alice had got so much into the way of expecting nothing but out-of-the-way things to happen, that it seemed quite dull and stupid for life to go on in the common way.

So she set to work, and very soon finished off the cake.

*   *   *

*   *   *   *

*   *   *

"Eat Me" Cakes

WITH BLACKCURRANT ICING

All cakes are trying to tell you something.
Some cakes say things like "Happy Birthday" or "Congratulations,"
but if you read between the lines they all say "Eat Me."

Makes about 18 cupcakes

Ingredients

CAKE

½ cup (125 mL) butter, softened

1⅓ cups (325 mL) sugar

2 large eggs

2 tsp (10 mL) vanilla

2 cups (500 mL) all-purpose
    flour

1 tsp (5 mL) baking powder

1 tsp (5 mL) baking soda

½ tsp (2 mL) salt

1 cup (250 mL) buttermilk

1 cup (250 mL) fresh or frozen
    blackcurrants (optional)

BLACKCURRANT ICING

4–5 cups (1–1.25 L) icing sugar

¼ cup (60 mL) light corn syrup
    or golden syrup

¼ cup (60 mL) water or
    blackcurrant concentrate

¼ tsp (1 mL) vanilla

Alice's advice

Spell "Eat Me" on your cakes
in extra blackcurrants, or if you
have none, stir water or bottled
blackcurrant concentrate into
icing sugar until you have a
squeezable consistency. Spoon
the icing into a small Ziplock
bag and snip a teeny bit off one
corner. Gently squeeze the icing
out while writing.

Preheat the oven to 400°F (200°C) and butter two 8-inch (20 cm)
or 9-inch (23 cm) round cake pans.

TO MAKE THE CAKE In a large bowl, beat the butter and sugar for
a few minutes, until pale and fluffy. Beat in the eggs and vanilla.

In a small bowl, stir together the flour, baking powder, baking
soda and salt.

By hand or with the mixer on low speed, add the flour mixture
to the butter mixture in 3 batches, alternating with buttermilk,
beginning and ending with the flour and mixing after each
addition just until combined.

Divide the batter between the pans and if you like, scatter
blackcurrants overtop.

Bake for 25 to 30 minutes, until golden and springy to the
touch. Invert onto wire racks to cool completely, then cut into
small rounds or squares using a 1½-inch (4 cm) round cookie
cutter or a knife.

TO MAKE THE BLACKCURRANT ICING Whisk all the ingredients
together in a double boiler set over simmering water. When
warm and smooth, remove from heat and set aside to cool for
about 10 minutes.

Place the cut-out cakes on a wire rack and pour the icing slowly
and evenly over them, coating them completely. If the icing cools
and gets too thick, rewarm it a bit.

If you like, top with fresh blackcurrants and allow the cakes
to set. Otherwise, let the icing set before writing on top (see Alice's
advice).

Makes about 18 little cakes, and lots of scraps to nibble. This
recipe is easily doubled if you expect many guests for tea.

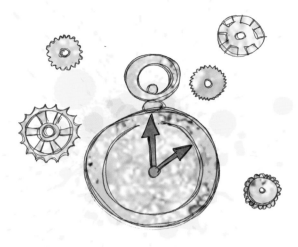

CHAPTER 2

The Pool of Tears

"Curiouser and curiouser!" cried Alice (she was so much surprised, that for the moment she quite forgot how to speak good English). "Now I'm opening out like the largest telescope that ever was! Good-bye, feet!" (for when she looked down at her feet, they seemed to be almost out of sight, they were getting so far off). "Oh, my poor little feet, I wonder who will put on your shoes and stockings for you now, dears? I'm sure *I* shan't be able! I shall be a great deal too far off to trouble myself about you: you must manage the best way you can—but I must be kind to them," thought Alice, "or perhaps they won't walk the way I want to go! Let me see. I'll give them a new pair of boots every Christmas."

And she went on planning to herself how she would manage it. "They must go by the carrier," she thought; "and how funny it'll seem, sending presents to one's own feet! And how odd the directions will look!

> Alice's Right Foot, Esq.,
> Hearthrug,
>   near the Fender,
>   (with Alice's love).

Oh dear, what nonsense I'm talking!"

Just at this moment her head struck against the roof of the hall: in fact she was now rather more than nine feet high, and she at once took up the little golden key and hurried off to the garden door.

Poor Alice! It was as much as she could do, lying down on one side, to look through into the garden with one eye; but to get through was more hopeless than ever: she sat down and began to cry again.

"You ought to be ashamed of yourself," said Alice, "a great girl like you," (she might well say this), "to go on crying in this way! Stop this moment, I tell you!" But she went on all the same, shedding gallons of tears, until there was a large pool all round her, about four inches deep and reaching half down the hall.

After a time she heard a little pattering of feet in the distance, and she hastily dried her eyes to see what was coming. It was the White Rabbit returning, splendidly dressed, with a pair of white kid gloves in one hand and a large fan in the other: he came trotting along in a great hurry, muttering to himself as he came, "Oh! the Duchess, the Duchess! Oh! *won't* she be savage if I've kept her waiting!" Alice felt so desperate that she was ready to ask help of any one: so, when the Rabbit came near her, she began, in a low, timid voice, "If you please, sir—" The Rabbit started violently, dropped the white kid gloves and the fan, and skurried away into the darkness as hard as he could go.

Alice took up the fan and gloves, and, as the hall was very hot, she kept fanning herself all the time she went on talking. "Dear, dear! How queer everything is to-day! And yesterday things went on just as usual. I wonder if I've been changed in the night? Let me think: *was* I the same when I got up this morning? I almost think I can remember feeling a little different. But if I'm not the same, the next question is, 'Who in the world am I?' Ah, *that's* the great puzzle!" And she began thinking over all the children she knew that were of the same age as herself, to see if she could have been changed for any of them.

"I'm sure I'm not Ada," she said, "for her hair goes in such long ringlets, and mine doesn't go in ringlets at all; and I'm sure I can't be Mabel, for I know all sorts of things, and she, oh, she knows such a very little! Besides, *she's* she, and *I'm* I, and—oh dear, how

WHITE RABBIT'S

White chocolate

POT DE CRÈME

White Chocolate

POT DE CRÈME

Difficult times go much smoother when you're not in such
a tremendous flustery rush. Take the time to enjoy a pot de crème,
a silky sweet, luscious chocolate custard that is like a crème brulée
without the crackly burnt-sugar top.

Fills 6 little pots

Ingredients

2 cups (500 mL) heavy
  (whipping) cream or 18%
  cream

1 cup (250 mL) white chocolate,
  chopped (about 4 oz/120 g)

6 large egg yolks

2 Tbsp (30 mL) sugar

Preheat the oven to 325°F and set a rack in the middle. Arrange
five or six ¾-cup (185 mL) ramekins in a 9- × 13-inch (3.5 L) pan.

In a medium saucepan, heat the cream over medium heat until
it's steaming; remove from the heat and add the chocolate. Let it
sit for a few minutes, then whisk until it's melted and smooth.

In a medium bowl, whisk together the egg yolks and sugar.
When the chocolate mixture has cooled to warm—enough so that
it won't cook the eggs—whisk it into the egg mixture. Divide the
custard between the ramekins, and pour enough warm water into
the pan to come halfway up the sides of the cups.

Bake for 30 to 40 minutes, or until the custards are set but still
just slightly jiggly in the middle. Cool, then cover each ramekin
with plastic wrap and refrigerate until well chilled—at least 2
hours, or up to a day.

puzzling it all is! I'll try if I know all the things I used to know. Let me see: four times five is twelve, and four times six is thirteen, and four times seven is—oh dear! I shall never get to twenty at that rate! However, the Multiplication Table doesn't signify: let's try Geography. London is the capital of Paris, and Paris is the capital of Rome, and Rome—no, *that's* all wrong, I'm certain! I must have been changed for Mabel! I'll try and say '*How doth the little*—' and she crossed her hands on her lap as if she were saying lessons, and began to repeat it, but her voice sounded hoarse and strange, and the words did not come the same as they used to do:—

> "How doth the little crocodile
>   Improve his shining tail,
> And pour the waters of the Nile
>   On every golden scale!

> "How cheerfully he seems to grin,
>   How neatly spread his claws,
> And welcomes little fishes in
>   With gently smiling jaws!"

"I'm sure those are not the right words," said poor Alice, and her eyes filled with tears again as she went on, "I must be Mabel after all, and I shall have to go and live in that poky little house, and have next to no toys to play with, and oh, ever so many lessons to learn! No, I've made up my mind about it: if I'm Mabel, I'll stay down here! It'll be no use their putting their heads down and saying, "Come up again, dear!" I shall only look up and say, "Who am I, then? Tell me that first, and then, if I like being that person, I'll come up: if not, I'll stay down here till I'm somebody else"—but, oh dear!" cried Alice, with a sudden burst of tears, "I do wish they *would* put their heads down! I am so *very* tired of being all alone here!"

As she said this, she looked down at her hands, and was surprised to see that she had put on one of the Rabbit's little white kid gloves while she was talking. "How *can* I have done that?" she thought. "I must be growing small again." She got up and went to the table to measure herself by it, and found that, as nearly as she could guess, she was now about two feet high, and was going on shrinking rapidly:

she soon found out that the cause of this was the fan she was holding, and she dropped it hastily, just in time to save herself from shrinking away altogether.

"That *was* a narrow escape!" said Alice, a good deal frightened at the sudden change, but very glad to find herself still in existence. "And now for the garden!" And she ran with all speed back to the little door; but, alas! the little door was shut again, and the little golden key was lying on the glass table as before, "and things are worse than ever," thought the poor child, "for I never was so small as this before, never! And I declare it's too bad, that it is!"

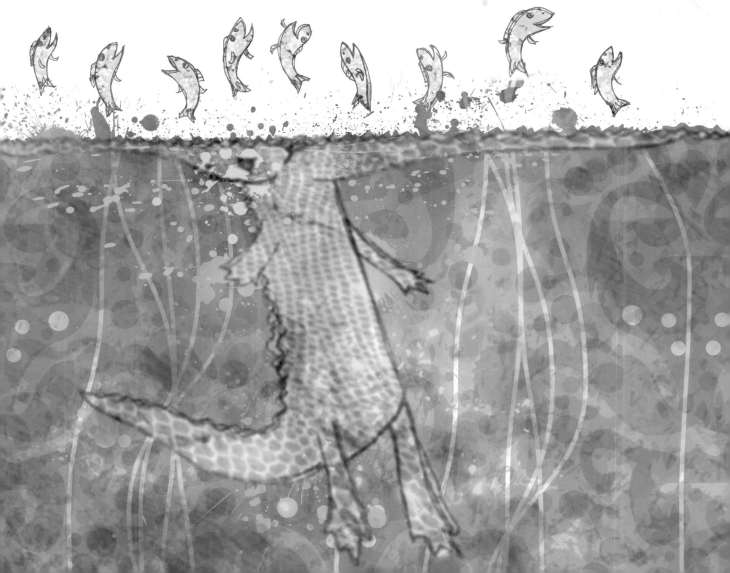

As she said these words her foot slipped, and in another moment, splash! she was up to her chin in salt water. Her first idea was that she had somehow fallen into the sea, "and in that case I can go back by railway," she said to herself. (Alice had been to the seaside once in her life, and had come to the general conclusion that, wherever you go to on the English coast, you find a number of bathing machines in the sea, some children digging in the sand with wooden spades, then a row of lodging houses, and behind them a railway station.) However, she soon made out that she was in the pool of tears which she had wept when she was nine feet high.

"I wish I hadn't cried so much!" said Alice, as she swam about, trying to find her way out. "I shall be punished for it now, I suppose, by being drowned in my own tears! That *will* be a queer thing, to be sure! However, everything is queer to-day."

Just then she heard something splashing about in the pool a little way off, and she swam nearer to make out what it was: at first she thought it must be a walrus or hippopotamus, but then she remembered how small she was now, and she soon made out that it was only a mouse that had slipped in like herself.

"Would it be of any use, now," thought Alice, "to speak to this mouse? Everything is so out-of-the-way down here, that I should think very likely it can talk: at any rate, there's no harm in trying." So she began: "O Mouse, do you know the way out of this pool? I am very tired of swimming about here, O Mouse!" (Alice thought this must be the right way of speaking to a mouse: she had never done such a thing before, but she remembered having seen in her brother's Latin Grammar, "A mouse—of a mouse—to a mouse—a mouse—O mouse!" The Mouse looked at her rather inquisitively, and seemed to her to wink with one of its little eyes, but it said nothing.

"Perhaps it doesn't understand English," thought Alice. "I daresay it's a French mouse, come over with William the Conqueror." (For, with all her knowledge of history, Alice had no very clear notion how long ago anything had happened.) So she began again: "Où est ma chatte?" which was the first sentence in her French lesson-book. The Mouse gave a sudden leap out of the water, and seemed to quiver all over with fright. "Oh, I beg your pardon!" cried Alice hastily, afraid that she had hurt the poor animal's feelings. "I quite forgot you didn't like cats."

ALICE'S

Salted
caramel

TEARDROPS

Salted Caramel

Pretzel sticks dipped in homemade caramel are a curious combination of sweet, salty, crunchy and chewy. They might make you exclaim something like "Curiouser and curiouser!" and even if that is not proper English, you would not be wrong.

Makes about 100 caramel-dipped pretzel sticks

Ingredients

½ cup (125 mL) corn syrup
    or golden syrup

1 cup (250 mL) sugar

½ tsp (2 mL) salt

¼ tsp (1 mL) lemon juice

1 cup (250 mL) heavy
    (whipping) cream

1 Tbsp (15 mL) butter

1 tsp (5 mL) vanilla

10 oz/400 g (about ½ a bag)
    salted pretzel sticks

Alice's advice

Rather than dip pretzel sticks, you could cut caramel pieces. Pour the caramel into a 9-inch (23 cm) square pan lined with foil and buttered. Let set for an hour or so, until slightly firm but still tacky. Sprinkle the surface lightly with flaky salt, pressing gently to help it adhere, and leave for another 3 to 4 hours, until firm. Remove the whole block of caramel and cut it into small squares on a cutting board. Wrap each caramel individually in waxed paper or cellophane.

In a large, heavy-bottomed saucepan, heat the syrup, sugar, salt and lemon juice over medium-high heat, stirring until the sugar dissolves completely and the mixture begins to simmer around the edges. At this point, stop stirring—you can swirl the pan as the temperature rises.

Cook uncovered, swirling the pan occasionally, until the mixture reaches 305°F (150°C) on a candy thermometer. Meanwhile, warm the cream in a small saucepan.

When the sugar mixture reaches 305°F (150°C), remove the pan from the heat and stir in the butter. Gradually stir in the hot cream; it will bubble up and steam, so be careful. It will clump up as some of the caramel solidifies—don't worry about this. Return the pan to the heat and cook, stirring occasionally at the beginning and more frequently at the end, for about 15 minutes, or until the mixture is smooth and reaches 260°F (125°C) on the candy thermometer.

Remove the pan from the heat and stir in the vanilla. Set it aside for 5 minutes or so, until it thickens to the texture of thick molasses.

Dip each pretzel stick a third to halfway deep, swirling to catch drips and coat the end of each pretzel, then set on a parchment-lined baking sheet and let sit until cool. If the caramel thickens to the point where you can't dip the pretzels anymore, warm it again over low heat. If you like, shape the soft caramel around the end of each pretzel when it cools enough to handle but is still pliable.

"Not like cats!" cried the Mouse, in a shrill, passionate voice. "Would *you* like cats if you were me?"

"Well, perhaps not," said Alice in a soothing tone: "don't be angry about it. And yet I wish I could show you our cat Dinah. I think you'd take a fancy to cats, if you could only see her. She is such a dear quiet thing," Alice went on, half to herself, as she swam lazily about in the pool, "and she sits purring so nicely by the fire, licking her paws and washing her face—and she is such a nice soft thing to nurse—and she's such a capital one for catching mice—oh, I beg your pardon!" cried Alice again, for this time the Mouse was bristling all over, and she felt certain it must be really offended. "We won't talk about her any more if you'd rather not."

"We, indeed!" cried the Mouse, who was trembling down to the end of his tail. "As if *I* would talk on such a subject! Our family always *hated* cats: nasty, low, vulgar things! Don't let me hear the name again!"

"I won't indeed!" said Alice, in a great hurry to change the subject of conversation. "Are you—are you fond—of—of dogs?" The Mouse did not answer, so Alice went on eagerly: "There is such a nice little dog, near our house, I should like

to show you! A little bright-eyed terrier, you know, with oh, such long curly brown hair! And it'll fetch things when you throw them, and it'll sit up and beg for its dinner, and all sorts of things—I can't remember half of them—and it belongs to a farmer, you know, and he says it's so useful, it's worth a hundred pounds! He says it kills all the rats and—oh dear!" cried Alice in a sorrowful tone, "I'm afraid I've offended it again!" For the Mouse was swimming away from her as hard as it could go, and making quite a commotion in the pool as it went.

So she called softly after it, "Mouse dear! Do come back again, and we won't talk about cats, or dogs either, if you don't like them!" When the Mouse heard this, it turned round and swam slowly back to her: its face was quite pale (with passion, Alice thought), and it said, in a low, trembling voice, "Let us get to the shore, and then I'll tell you my history, and you'll understand why it is I hate cats and dogs."

It was high time to go, for the pool was getting quite crowded with the birds and animals that had fallen into it: there were a Duck and a Dodo, a Lory and an Eaglet, and several other curious creatures. Alice led the way, and the whole party swam to the shore.

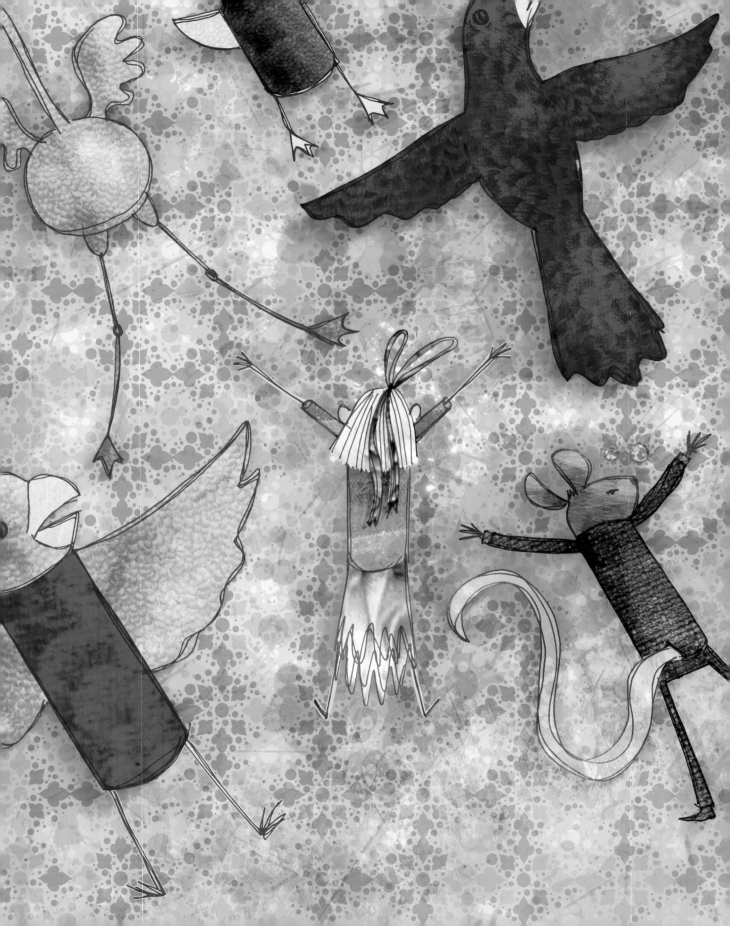

CHAPTER 3

A Caucus-Race and a Long Tale

They were indeed a queer-looking party that assembled on the bank—the birds with draggled feathers, the animals with their fur clinging close to them, and all dripping wet, cross, and uncomfortable.

The first question of course was, how to get dry again: they had a consultation about this, and after a few minutes it seemed quite natural to Alice to find herself talking familiarly with them, as if she had known them all her life. Indeed, she had quite a long argument with the Lory, who at last turned sulky, and would only say, "I am older than you, and must know better." And this Alice would not allow, without knowing how old it was, and, as the Lory positively refused to tell its age, there was no more to be said.

At last the Mouse, who seemed to be a person of some authority among them, called out, "Sit down, all of you, and listen to me! *I'll* soon make you dry enough!" They all sat down at once, in a large ring, with the Mouse in the middle. Alice kept her eyes anxiously fixed on it, for she felt sure she would catch a bad cold if she did not get dry very soon.

"Ahem!" said the Mouse with an important air. "Are you all ready? This is the driest thing I know. Silence all round, if you please! 'William the Conqueror, whose cause was favoured by the pope, was soon submitted to by the English, who wanted leaders, and had been of late much accustomed to usurpation and conquest. Edwin and Morcar, the earls of Mercia and Northumbria—'"

"Ugh!" said the Lory, with a shiver.

"I beg your pardon!" said the Mouse, frowning, but very politely. "Did you speak?"

"Not I!" said the Lory hastily.

"I thought you did," said the Mouse. "—I proceed. "'Edwin and Morcar, the earls of Mercia and Northumbria, declared for him; and even Stigand, the patriotic archbishop of Canterbury, found it advisable—'"

"Found *what*?" said the Duck.

"Found *it*," the Mouse replied rather crossly: "of course you know what 'it' means."

"I know what 'it' means well enough, when *I* find a thing," said the Duck: "it's generally a frog or a worm. The question is, what did the archbishop find?"

The Mouse did not notice this question, but hurriedly went on, "'—found it advisable to go with Edgar Atheling to meet William and offer him the crown. William's conduct at first was moderate. But the insolence of his Normans—'" How are you getting on now, my dear?" it continued, turning to Alice as it spoke.

"As wet as ever," said Alice in a melancholy tone: "it doesn't seem to dry me at all."

"In that case," said the Dodo solemnly, rising to its feet, "I move that the meeting adjourn, for the immediate adoption of more energetic remedies—"

"Speak English!" said the Eaglet. "I don't know the meaning of half those long words, and, what's more, I don't believe you do either!" And the Eaglet bent down its head to hide a smile: some of the other birds tittered audibly.

"What I was going to say," said the Dodo in an offended tone, "was, that the best thing to get us dry would be a Caucus-race."

"What *is* a Caucus-race?" said Alice; not that she much wanted to know, but the Dodo had paused as if it thought that *somebody* ought to speak, and no one else seemed inclined to say anything.

"Why," said the Dodo, "the best way to explain it is to do it." (And, as you might like to try the thing yourself, some winter day, I will tell you how the Dodo managed it.)

First it marked out a race-course, in a sort of circle ("the exact shape doesn't matter," it said), and then all the party were placed along the course, here and there. There was no "One, two, three, and away!" but they began running when they liked, and left off when they liked, so that it was not easy to know when the race was over. However, when they had been running half-an-hour or so, and were quite dry again, the Dodo suddenly called out "The race is over!" and they all crowded round it, panting, and asking, "But who has won?"

This question the Dodo could not answer without a great deal of thought, and it stood for a long time with one finger pressed upon its forehead (the position in which you usually see Shakespeare, in the pictures of him), while the rest waited in silence. At last the Dodo said, "*Everybody* has won, and *all* must have prizes."

"But who is to give the prizes?" quite a chorus of voices asked.

"Why, *she*, of course," said the Dodo, pointing to Alice with one finger; and the whole party at once crowded round her, calling out, in a confused way, "Prizes! Prizes!"

Alice had no idea what to do, and in despair she put her hand in her pocket, and pulled out a box of comfits (luckily the salt water had not got into it), and handed them round as prizes. There was exactly one a-piece, all round.

"But she must have a prize herself, you know," said the Mouse.

"Of course," the Dodo replied very gravely. "What else have you got in your pocket?" it went on, turning to Alice.

"Only a thimble," said Alice sadly.

"Hand it over here," said the Dodo.

Then they all crowded round her once more, while the Dodo solemnly presented the thimble, saying, "We beg your acceptance of this elegant thimble"; and, when it had finished this short speech, they all cheered.

Alice thought the whole thing very absurd, but they all looked so grave that she did not dare to laugh; and, as she could not think of anything to say, she simply bowed, and took the thimble, looking as solemn as she could.

The next thing was to eat the comfits: this caused some noise and confusion, as the large birds complained that they could not taste theirs, and the small ones choked and had to be patted on the back. However, it was over at last, and they sat down again in a ring, and begged the Mouse to tell them something more.

ALICE'S
Prize-winning
MIXED-NUT
comfits

Prize-Winning Mixed-Nut Comfits

Ah, the sweet taste of victory. You will be the champion
of all the nuts you run with when you make your very own
comfits, candy-coated, nutty confections. Everybody wins
when you celebrate life's little victories.

Makes about 2½ cups (625 mL)

Ingredients

- 2 cups (500 mL) whole almonds, walnuts, pecans or a combination
- 3 Tbsp (45 mL) honey
- 2 Tbsp (30 mL) water
- 1 Tbsp (15 mL) butter
- ¼ cup (60 mL) sugar
- ½ tsp (2 mL) salt
- ¼ tsp (1 mL) cinnamon (optional)

In a large, heavy skillet set over medium-high heat, toast the nuts for 3 to 4 minutes, until they are starting to turn fragrant. Add the honey, water and butter and cook, stirring, for another 3 to 4 minutes, until the syrupy mixture has been almost absorbed by the nuts and there isn't much left in the pan.

Stir in the sugar, salt and cinnamon, if you're using it, and stir to coat well. Remove from the heat and spread out in a single layer on a parchment- or foil-lined sheet; set aside to cool. Break apart, into pieces, and serve in a bowl or small paper cups.

"You promised to tell me your history, you know," said Alice, "and why it is you hate—C and D," she added in a whisper, half afraid that it would be offended again.

"Mine is a long and a sad tale!" said the Mouse, turning to Alice, and sighing.

"It *is* a long tail, certainly," said Alice, looking down with wonder at the Mouse's tail; "but why do you call it sad?" And she kept on puzzling about it while the Mouse was speaking, so that her idea of the tale was something like this:—

"Fury said to a mouse, That he met in the house, 'Let us both go to law: I will prosecute you.—Come, I'll take no denial; We must have a trial: For really this morning I've nothing to do.' Said the mouse to the cur, 'Such a trial, dear sir, With no jury or judge, would be wasting our breath.' 'I'll be judge, I'll be jury,' Said cunning old Fury; 'I'll try the whole cause, and condemn you to death.'"

"You are not attending!" said the Mouse to Alice, severely. "What are you thinking of?"

"I beg your pardon," said Alice very humbly: "you had got to the fifth bend, I think?"

"I had *not*!" cried the Mouse, sharply and very angrily.

"A knot!" said Alice, all ready to make herself useful, and looking anxiously about her. "Oh, do let me help to undo it!"

"I shall do nothing of the sort," said the Mouse, getting up and walking away. "You insult me by talking such nonsense!"

"I didn't mean it!" pleaded poor Alice. "But you're so easily offended, you know!"

The Mouse only growled in reply.

"Please come back, and finish your story!" Alice called after it. And the others all joined in chorus "Yes, please do!" but the Mouse only shook its head impatiently, and walked a little quicker.

"What a pity it wouldn't stay!" sighed the Lory, as soon as it was quite out of sight. And an old Crab took the opportunity of saying to her daughter, "Ah, my dear! Let this be a lesson to you never to lose *your* temper!" "Hold your tongue, Ma!" said the young Crab, a little snappishly. "You're enough to try the patience of an oyster!"

"I wish I had our Dinah here, I know I do!" said Alice aloud, addressing nobody in particular. "*She'd* soon fetch it back!"

"And who is Dinah, if I might venture to ask the question?" said the Lory.

Alice replied eagerly, for she was always ready to talk about her pet: "Dinah's our cat. And she's such a capital one for catching mice, you can't think! And oh, I wish you could see her after the birds! Why, she'll eat a little bird as soon as look at it!"

This speech caused a remarkable sensation among the party. Some of the birds hurried off at once: one old Magpie began wrapping itself up very carefully, remarking, "I really must be getting home: the night-air doesn't suit my throat!" and a Canary called out in a trembling voice, to its children, "Come away, my dears! It's high time you were all in bed!" On various pretexts they all moved off, and Alice was soon left alone.

"I wish I hadn't mentioned Dinah!" she said to herself in a melancholy tone. "Nobody seems to like her, down here, and I'm sure she's the best cat in the world! Oh, my dear Dinah! I wonder if I shall ever see you any more!" And here poor Alice began to cry again, for she felt very lonely and low-spirited. In a little while, however, she again heard a little pattering of footsteps in the distance, and she looked up eagerly, half hoping that the Mouse had changed his mind, and was coming back to finish his story.

CHAPTER 4

Rabbit Sends in a Little Bill

t was the White Rabbit, trotting slowly back again, and looking anxiously about as it went, as if it had lost something; and she heard it muttering to itself, "The Duchess! The Duchess! Oh my dear paws! Oh my fur and whiskers! She'll get me executed, as sure as ferrets are ferrets! Where *can* I have dropped them, I wonder?" Alice guessed in a moment that it was looking for the fan and the pair of white kid gloves, and she very good-naturedly began hunting about for them, but they were nowhere to be seen—everything seemed to have changed since her swim in the pool, and the great hall, with the glass table and the little door, had vanished completely.

Very soon the Rabbit noticed Alice, as she went hunting about, and called out to her, in an angry tone, "Why, Mary Ann, what *are* you doing out here? Run home this moment, and fetch me a pair of gloves and a fan! Quick, now!" And Alice was so much frightened that she ran off at once in the direction it pointed to, without trying to explain the mistake it had made.

"He took me for his housemaid," she said to herself as she ran. "How surprised he'll be when he finds out who I am! But I'd better take him his fan and gloves—that is, if I can find them." As she said this, she came upon a neat little house, on

the door of which was a bright brass plate with the name "W. RABBIT," engraved upon it. She went in without knocking, and hurried upstairs, in great fear lest she should meet the real Mary Ann, and be turned out of the house before she had found the fan and gloves.

"How queer it seems," Alice said to herself, "to be going messages for a rabbit! I suppose Dinah'll be sending me on messages next!" And she began fancying the sort of thing that would happen: "'Miss Alice! Come here directly, and get ready for your walk!' 'Coming in a minute, nurse! But I've got to watch this mouse-hole till Dinah comes back and see that the mouse doesn't get out.' Only I don't think," Alice went on, "that they'd let Dinah stop in the house if it began ordering people about like that!"

By this time she had found her way into a tidy little room with a table in the window, and on it (as she had hoped) a fan and two or three pairs of tiny white kid gloves: she took up the fan and a pair of the gloves, and was just going to leave the room, when her eye fell upon a little bottle that stood near the looking-glass. There was no label this time with the words "DRINK ME," but nevertheless she uncorked it and put it to her lips. "I know *something* interesting is sure to happen," she said to herself, "whenever I eat or drink anything: so I'll just see what this bottle does. I do hope it'll make me grow large again, for really I'm quite tired of being such a tiny little thing!"

It did so indeed, and much sooner than she had expected: before she had drunk half the bottle, she found her head pressing against the ceiling, and had to stoop to save her neck from being broken. She hastily put down the bottle, saying to herself, "That's quite enough—I hope I shan't grow any more—As it is, I can't get out at the door—I do wish I hadn't drunk quite so much!"

Alas! it was too late to wish that! She went on growing and growing, and very soon had to kneel down on the floor: in another minute there was not even room for this, and she tried the effect of lying down with one elbow against the door, and the other arm curled round her head. Still she went on growing, and, as a last resource, she put one arm out of the window, and one foot up the chimney, and said to herself "Now I can do no more, whatever happens. What *will* become of me?"

Luckily for Alice, the little magic bottle had now had its full effect, and she grew no larger: still it was very uncomfortable, and, as there seemed to be no sort

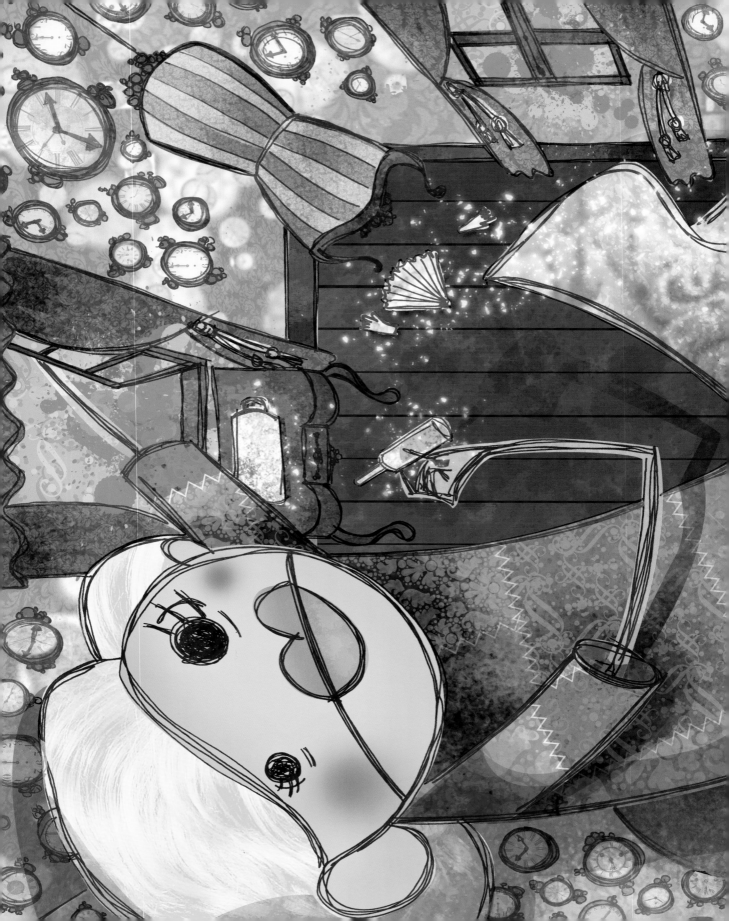

of chance of her ever getting out of the room again, no wonder she felt unhappy.

"It was much pleasanter at home," thought poor Alice, "when one wasn't always growing larger and smaller, and being ordered about by mice and rabbits. I almost wish I hadn't gone down that rabbit-hole—and yet—and yet—it's rather curious, you know, this sort of life! I do wonder what *can* have happened to me! When I used to read fairy-tales, I fancied that kind of thing never happened, and now here I am in the middle of one! There ought to be a book written about me, that there ought! And when I grow up, I'll write one—but I'm grown up now," she added in a sorrowful tone: "at least there's no room to grow up any more *here*."

"But then," thought Alice, "shall I *never* get any older than I am now? That'll be a comfort, one way—*never* to be an old woman— but then—always to have lessons to learn! Oh, I shouldn't like *that*!"

"Oh, you foolish Alice!" she answered herself. "How can you learn lessons in here? Why, there's hardly room for *you*, and no room at all for any lesson-books!"

And so she went on, taking first one side and then the other, and making quite a conversation of it altogether; but after a few minutes she heard a voice outside, and stopped to listen.

"Mary Ann! Mary Ann!" said the voice. "Fetch me my gloves this moment!" Then came a little pattering of feet on the stairs. Alice knew it was the Rabbit coming to look for her, and she trembled till she shook the house, quite forgetting that she was now about a thousand times as large as the Rabbit, and had no reason to be afraid of it.

Presently the Rabbit came up to the door, and tried to open it; but, as the door opened inwards, and Alice's elbow was pressed hard against it, that attempt proved a failure. Alice heard it say to itself, "Then I'll go round and get in at the window."

"*That* you won't!" thought Alice, and, after waiting till she fancied she heard the Rabbit just under the window, she suddenly spread out her hand, and made a snatch in the air. She did not get hold of anything, but she heard a little shriek and a fall, and a crash of broken glass, from which she concluded that it was just possible it had fallen into a cucumber-frame, or something of the sort.

Next came an angry voice—the Rabbit's—"Pat! Pat! Where are you?" And then a voice she had never heard before, "Sure then I'm here! Digging for apples, yer honour!"

"Digging for apples, indeed!" said the Rabbit angrily. "Here! Come and help me out of *this*!" (Sounds of more broken glass.)

"Now tell me, Pat, what's that in the window?"

"Sure, it's an arm, yer honour!" (He pronounced it "arrum.")

"An arm, you goose! Who ever saw one that size? Why, it fills the whole window!"

"Sure, it does, yer honour: but it's an arm for all that."

"Well, it's got no business there, at any rate: go and take it away!"

There was a long silence after this, and Alice could only hear whispers now and then; such as, "Sure, I don't like it, yer honour, at all, at all!" "Do as I tell you, you coward!" and at last she spread out her hand again, and made another snatch in the air. This time there were *two* little shrieks, and more sounds of broken glass. "What a number of cucumber-frames there must be!" thought Alice. "I wonder what they'll do next! As for pulling me out of the window, I only wish they *could*! I'm sure I don't want to stay in here any longer!"

She waited for some time without hearing anything more: at last came a rumbling of little cartwheels, and the sound of a good many voices all talking together: she made out the words: "Where's the other ladder?—Why, I hadn't to

Cucumber Frames

The life of a cucumber is generally spent indoors and hence
it develops the refined sophistication of English gentlefolk. Cucumbers
love to read books and fill their minds with lots of different fillings . . .

Makes about 2 dozen cucumber frames

Ingredients

2 long English cucumbers

CREAMY CRAB OR SHRIMP FILLING

one 4 oz (120 g) can crabmeat
   or cocktail shrimp

1 pkg (8 oz/250 g) cream
   cheese, at room temperature

¼ cup (60 mL) mayonnaise

1 green onion, finely chopped

1 Tbsp (15 mL) chili sauce
   or 1 tsp (5 mL) prepared
   horseradish

2 tsp (10 mL) chopped fresh dill
   or parsley

2 tsp (10 mL) lemon juice

salt and ground black pepper
   to taste

SPINACH & ARTICHOKE FILLING

1 pkg (8 oz/250 g) cream
   cheese, at room temperature

2 Tbsp (30 mL) mayonnaise

1 garlic clove, crushed

one 4 oz (114 mL) jar marinated
   artichoke hearts, drained and
   coarsely chopped

½ pkg (5 oz/150 g) frozen
   spinach, thawed, squeezed
   dry and chopped

¼ cup (60 mL) freshly grated
   Parmesan cheese

salt and ground black pepper
   to taste

fresh parsley or dill, for garnish

HUMMUS FILLING

one 19 oz (540 mL) can
   chickpeas, drained

¼ cup (60 mL) tahini
   (sesame seed paste)

1 roasted red bell pepper
   (optional)

1 garlic clove, crushed

2 Tbsp (30 mL) lemon juice

2 Tbsp (30 mL) olive oil

salt and ground black pepper
   to taste

Cut stripes along the sides of the cucumber by peeling off strips
of skin using a vegetable peeler. Cut into ¾- to 1-inch (2–2.5 cm)
slices and, using a small spoon, scoop out enough of the innards to
form a small cup, leaving enough in the bottom to prevent drips.

To make the filling, combine your ingredients of choice in the
bowl of a food processor and pulse until well blended, and as rough
or smooth as you like. Fill each cucumber with a spoonful of filling,
and garnish with chopped fresh parsley or dill, if you like. Serve
immediately. (Make extra in case a rabbit decides to crash your
house party.)

bring but one; Bill's got the other—Bill! fetch it here, lad!—Here, put 'em up at this corner—No, tie 'em together first—they don't reach half high enough yet—Oh!, they'll do well enough. Don't be particular— Here, Bill! catch hold of this rope— Will the roof bear!?—Mind that loose slate—Oh, it's coming down! Heads below!" (a loud crash)—"Now, who did that?—It was Bill, I fancy—Who's to go down the chimney?—Nay, *I* shan't! *You* do it!—*That* I won't, then!—Bill's got to go down— Here, Bill! the master says you're to go down the chimney!"

"Oh! So Bill's got to come down the chimney, has he?" said Alice to herself. "Why, they seem to put everything upon Bill! I wouldn't be in Bill's place for a good deal; this fireplace is narrow, to be sure; but I *think* I can kick a little!"

She drew her foot as far down the chimney as she could, and waited till she heard a little animal (she couldn't guess of what sort it was) scratching and scrambling about in the chimney close above her: then, saying to herself "This is Bill," she gave one sharp kick, and waited to see what would happen next.

The first thing she heard was a general chorus of "There goes Bill!" then the Rabbit's voice along—"Catch him, you by the hedge!" then silence, and then another confusion of voices—"Hold up his head—Brandy now—Don't choke him—How was it, old fellow? What happened to you? Tell us all about it!"

Last came a little feeble, squeaking voice. ("That's Bill," thought Alice), "Well, I hardly know—No more, thank ye; I'm better now—but I'm a deal too flustered to tell you—all I know is, something comes at me like a Jack-in-the-box, and up I goes like a sky-rocket!"

"So you did, old fellow!" said the others.

"We must burn the house down!" said the Rabbit's voice, and Alice called out as loud as she could, "If you do, I'll set Dinah at you!"

There was a dead silence instantly, and Alice thought to herself, "I wonder what they *will* do next! If they had any sense, they'd take the roof off." After a minute or two, they began moving about again, and Alice heard the Rabbit say, "A barrowful will do, to begin with."

"A barrowful of *what*?" thought Alice. But she had not long to doubt, for the next moment a shower of little pebbles came rattling in at the window, and some of them hit her in the face. "I'll put a stop to this," she said to herself, and shouted out, "You'd better not do that again!" which produced another dead silence.

Alice noticed, with some surprise, that the pebbles were all turning into little cakes as they lay on the floor, and a bright idea came into her head. "If I eat one of these cakes," she thought, "it's sure to make *some* change in my size; and as it can't possibly make me larger, it must make me smaller, I suppose."

Brandy Snap-to-Its

To resuscitate someone who happens to be too flustered to talk after
a recent misfortune, do them the tremendous favour of giving them
something with brandy and ginger to help them snap back to it.

Makes about 2 dozen cookies for non-medical non-emergencies

Ingredients

½ cup (125 mL) butter, at room
temperature

1 cup (250 mL) sugar

½ cup (125 mL) brown sugar

¼ cup (60 mL) molasses

1 large egg

2 tsp (10 mL) brandy or
vanilla extract

2 cups (500 mL) all-purpose
flour

2 tsp (10 mL) baking soda

1 tsp (5 mL) cinnamon

1 tsp (5 mL) ginger

¼ tsp (1 mL) salt

extra sugar, for rolling

Preheat the oven to 325°F (160°C). In a large bowl, beat the butter,
sugar and brown sugar for 2 minutes, until pale and light. Beat in
the molasses, egg and brandy.

In another bowl, whisk together the flour, baking soda,
cinnamon, ginger and salt. Add to the butter mixture and stir until
you have a soft dough.

Roll the dough into 1-inch (2.5 cm) balls and roll in a shallow
dish of sugar to coat. Place 1 to 2 inches (2.5–5 cm) apart on a
parchment-lined baking sheet. Bake for 12 to 15 minutes, until
crackled, golden around the edges and set. If you want them extra
snappy, bake for another 2 to 3 minutes.

Using a thin spatula, transfer the cookies to a wire rack to cool.

ALICE'S Little cake pebbles

Little Cake Pebbles

People who live in glass houses should not throw pebbles.
Instead, they should throw parties with cake pebbles that are chocolate
coated and crunchy on the outside, with soft, sweet and cakey insides.
A barrowful will do, to begin with.

Makes 3 to 4 dozen cake pebbles

Ingredients

- 1 pkg (8 oz/250 g) cream cheese, at room temperature
- ¼ cup (60 mL) butter, at room temperature
- 3 cups (750 mL) icing sugar
- 2–3 Tbsp (30–45 mL) milk, half and half or 18% cream
- 2 baked cake layers or pound cakes, any flavour
- 1 lb (454 g) milk, dark or white chocolate, chopped, or candy melts, any colour

In a large bowl, beat the cream cheese and butter until smooth and creamy; beat in the icing sugar and milk until smooth. It will have the consistency of soft frosting.

Crumble the cakes finely into the frosting, and stir until well blended. Cover and refrigerate for at least an hour, or overnight.

Roll the mixture into 1-inch (2.5 cm) balls, making them a little imperfect so they resemble pebbles. Place them on a parchment-lined baking sheet, and place the sheet back into the fridge or freezer while you melt the chocolate.

Melt the chocolate on low heat in the microwave or in a double boiler set over simmering water, stirring until smooth.

If you want the pebbles to be on sticks, poke a lollipop stick into each ball, and use it to dip each into the warm chocolate, turning to coat. Otherwise, use a fork or bamboo skewer to hold each ball as you dip. Set the dipped balls on waxed or parchment paper. If you like, sprinkle with candy sprinkles, coconut, finely chopped nuts, coloured sugar or other decorations before the chocolate sets.

Let the cake pebbles sit at room temperature or refrigerate until firm.

So she swallowed one of the cakes, and was delighted to find that she began shrinking directly. As soon as she was small enough to get through the door, she ran out of the house, and found quite a crowd of little animals and birds waiting outside. The poor little Lizard, Bill, was in the middle, being held up by two guinea-pigs, who were giving it something out of a bottle. They all made a rush at Alice the moment she appeared; but she ran off as hard as she could, and soon found herself safe in a thick wood.

"The first thing I've got to do," said Alice to herself, as she wandered about in the wood, "is to grow to my right size again; and the second thing is to find my way into that lovely garden. I think that will be the best plan."

It sounded an excellent plan, no doubt, and very neatly and simply arranged: the only difficulty was, that she had not the smallest idea how to set about it; and while she was peering about anxiously among the trees, a little sharp bark just over her head made her look up in a great hurry.

An enormous puppy was looking down at her with large round eyes, and feebly stretching out one paw, trying to touch her. "Poor little thing!" said Alice, in a coaxing tone, and she tried hard to whistle to it; but she was terribly frightened all the time at the thought that it might be hungry, in which case it would be very likely to eat her up in spite of all her coaxing.

Hardly knowing what she did, she picked up a little bit of stick, and held it out to the puppy: whereupon the puppy jumped into the air off all its feet at once, with a yelp of delight, and rushed at the stick, and made believe to worry it: then Alice dodged behind a great thistle, to keep herself from being run over; and the moment she appeared on the other side, the puppy made another rush at the stick, and tumbled head over heels in its hurry to get hold of it: then Alice, thinking it was very like having a game of play with a cart-horse, and expecting every moment to be trampled under its feet, ran round the thistle again: then the puppy began a series of short charges at the stick, running a very little way forwards each time and a long way back, and barking hoarsely all the while, till at last it sat down a good way off, panting, with its tongue hanging out of its mouth, and its great eyes half shut.

This seemed to Alice a good opportunity for making her escape: so she set off at once, and ran till she was quite tired and out of breath, and till the puppy's bark sounded quite faint in the distance.

"And yet what a dear little puppy it was!" said Alice, as she leant against a buttercup to rest herself, and fanned herself with one of the leaves. "I should have liked teaching it tricks very much, if—if I'd only been the right size to do it! Oh dear! I'd nearly forgotten that I've got to grow up again! Let me see—how *is* it to be managed? I suppose I ought to eat or drink something or other; but the great question is, 'What?'"

The great question certainly was, "What?" Alice looked all round her at the flowers and the blades of grass, but she could not see anything that looked like the right thing to eat or drink under the circumstances. There was a large mushroom growing near her, about the same height as herself; and, when she had looked under it, and on both sides of it, and behind it, it occurred to her that she might as well look and see what was on the top of it.

She stretched herself up on tiptoe, and peeped over the edge of the mushroom, and her eyes immediately met those of a large blue caterpillar, that was sitting on the top, with its arms folded, quietly smoking a long hookah, and taking not the smallest notice of her or of anything else.

CHAPTER 5

Advice from a Caterpillar

The Caterpillar and Alice looked at each other for some time in silence: at last the Caterpillar took the hookah out of its mouth, and addressed her in a languid, sleepy voice.

"Who are *You*?" said the Caterpillar.

This was not an encouraging opening for a conversation. Alice replied, rather shyly, "I—I hardly know, Sir, just at present— at least I know who I *was* when I got up this morning, but I think I must have been changed several times since then."

"What do you mean by that?" said the Caterpillar, sternly. "Explain yourself!"

"I can't explain *myself,* I'm afraid, sir" said Alice, "because I'm not myself, you see."

"I don't see," said the Caterpillar.

"I'm afraid I can't put it more clearly," Alice replied very politely, "for I can't understand it myself, to begin with; and being so many different sizes in a day is very confusing."

"It isn't," said the Caterpillar.

"Well, perhaps you haven't found it so yet," said Alice; "but when you have to turn into a chrysalis—you will some day, you know—and then after that into a butterfly, I should think you'll feel it a little queer, won't you?"

"Not a bit," said the Caterpillar.

"Well, perhaps *your* feelings may be different," said Alice; "all I know is, it would feel very queer to *me*."

"You!" said the Caterpillar contemptuously. "Who are *you*?"

Which brought them back again to the beginning of the conversation. Alice felt a little irritated at the Caterpillar's making such *very* short remarks, and she drew herself up and said, very gravely, "I think you ought to tell me who *you* are, first."

"Why?" said the Caterpillar.

Here was another puzzling question; and, as Alice could not think of any good reason, and as the Caterpillar seemed to be in a *very* unpleasant state of mind, she turned away.

"Come back!" the Caterpillar called after her. "I've something important to say!"

This sounded promising, certainly. Alice turned and came back again.

"Keep your temper," said the Caterpillar.

"Is that all?" said Alice, swallowing down her anger as well as she could.

"No," said the Caterpillar.

Alice thought she might as well wait, as she had nothing else to do, and perhaps after all it might tell her something worth hearing. For some minutes it puffed away without speaking, but at last it unfolded its arms, took the hookah out of its mouth again, and said, "So you think you're changed, do you?"

"I'm afraid I am, Sir," said Alice. "I can't remember things as I used—and I don't keep the same size for ten minutes together!"

"Can't remember *what* things?" said the Caterpillar.

"Well, I've tried to say '*How doth the little busy bee*,' but it all came different!" Alice replied in a very melancholy voice.

"Repeat, '*You are old, Father William*,'" said the Caterpillar.

Alice folded her hands, and began:—

"You are old, Father William," the young man said,
"And your hair has become very white;
And yet you incessantly stand on your head—
Do you think, at your age, it is right?"

"In my youth," Father William replied to his son,
"I feared it might injure the brain;
But, now that I'm perfectly sure I have none,
Why, I do it again and again."

"You are old," said the youth, "as I mentioned before,
    And have grown most uncommonly fat;
Yet you turned a back-somersault in at the door—
    Pray, what is the reason of that?"

"In my youth," said the sage, as he shook his grey locks,
    "I kept all my limbs very supple
By the use of this ointment—one shilling the box—
    Allow me to sell you a couple?"

"You are old," said the youth, "and your jaws are too weak
For anything tougher than suet;
Yet you finished the goose, with the bones and the beak—
Pray how did you manage to do it?"

"In my youth," said his father, "I took to the law,
And argued each case with my wife;
And the muscular strength, which it gave to my jaw,
Has lasted the rest of my life."

"You are old," said the youth, "one would hardly suppose
That your eye was as steady as ever;
Yet you balanced an eel on the end of your nose—
What made you so awfully clever?"

"I have answered three questions, and that is enough,"
Said his father; "don't give yourself airs!
Do you think I can listen all day to such stuff?
Be off, or I'll kick you down stairs!"

"That is not said right," said the Caterpillar.

"Not *quite* right, I'm afraid," said Alice, timidly; "some of the words have got altered."

"It is wrong from beginning to end," said the Caterpillar decidedly; and there was silence for some minutes.

The Caterpillar was the first to speak.

"What size do you want to be?" it asked.

"Oh, I'm not particular as to size," Alice hastily replied; "only one doesn't like changing so often, you know."

"I *don't* know," said the Caterpillar.

Alice said nothing: she had never been so much contradicted in all her life before, and she felt that she was losing her temper.

"Are you content now?" said the Caterpillar.

"Well, I should like to be a *little* larger, Sir, if you wouldn't mind," said Alice: "three inches is such a wretched height to be."

"It is a very good height indeed!" said the Caterpillar angrily, rearing itself upright as it spoke (it was exactly three inches high).

CATERPILLAR'S DOUBLE-STUFFED Mushroom caps WITH TWO FILLING FLAVOURS

Double-Stuffed Mushroom Caps

WITH TWO FILLING FLAVOURS

One flavour will make you grow taller, and the other flavour
will make you grow shorter. To stay the same size,
you must eat one of each kind of stuffed mushroom cap.

Makes 24 mushrooms

Ingredients

2 dozen large white mushrooms

SAUSAGE STUFFING

1 Tbsp (15 mL) olive oil

1 Tbsp (15 mL) butter

1 large fresh Italian or chorizo
sausage

½ cup (125 mL) fresh
breadcrumbs

¼ cup (60 mL) freshly grated
Parmesan cheese

1 Tbsp (15 mL) finely chopped
parsley (optional)

RED BELL PEPPER & FETA
STUFFING

1 Tbsp (15 mL) olive oil

1 Tbsp (15 mL) butter

1 red bell pepper, seeded and
finely chopped

1 garlic clove, crushed

½ cup (125 mL) fresh
breadcrumbs

¼ cup (60 mL) finely crumbled
feta

1 Tbsp (15 mL) finely chopped
parsley (optional)

Preheat the oven to 350°F (180°C).

Remove the stems from the mushrooms. Set the caps aside
and roughly chop the stems.

TO MAKE THE SAUSAGE STUFFING Heat the oil and butter in
a medium skillet set over medium-high heat. Sauté half of the
chopped mushroom stems for 2 to 3 minutes, until soft. Squeeze
the sausage out of its casing into the pan and cook, breaking up
with a spoon, until the meat is well crumbled and no longer pink.
Transfer to a medium bowl and set aside to cool slightly. Add the
breadcrumbs, Parmesan and parsley (if using) to the bowl and
mix well.

TO MAKE THE RED BELL PEPPER & FETA STUFFING Heat the oil
and butter in a medium skillet set over medium-high heat. Sauté
the remaining chopped mushroom stems, bell pepper and garlic for
4 to 5 minutes, until soft and the excess moisture has cooked off.
Transfer to a medium bowl and set aside to cool slightly. Add the
breadcrumbs, feta and parsley (if using) to the bowl and mix well.

Use the stuffing mixture to stuff each mushroom cap, mounding
the mixture as much as possible and packing it in with your
fingers. Place stuffing-side up on a rimmed baking sheet and bake
for 20 minutes, until the mushrooms are soft and the filling is
crispy and golden.

Alice's advice

Try this with a big mushroom like a portobello if you find you are
growing and have a larger appetite. You will need to adjust to your
new size as best you can.

"But I'm not used to it!" pleaded poor Alice in a piteous tone. And she thought to herself, "I wish the creatures wouldn't be so easily offended!"

"You'll get used to it in time," said the Caterpillar; and it put the hookah into its mouth and began smoking again.

This time Alice waited patiently until it chose to speak again. In a minute or two the Caterpillar took the hookah out of its mouth and yawned once or twice, and shook itself. Then it got down off the mushroom, and crawled away into the grass, merely remarking, as it went, "One side will make you grow taller, and the other side will make you grow shorter."

"One side of *what*? The other side of *what*?" thought Alice to herself.

"Of the mushroom," said the Caterpillar, just as if she had asked it aloud; and in another moment it was out of sight.

Alice remained looking thoughtfully at the mushroom for a minute, trying to make out which were the two sides of it; and, as it was perfectly round, she found this a very difficult question. However, at last she stretched her arms round it as far as they would go, and broke off a bit of the edge with each hand.

"And now which is which?" she said to herself, and nibbled a little of the right-hand bit to try the effect. The next moment she felt a violent blow underneath her chin: it had struck her foot!

She was a good deal frightened by this very sudden change, but she felt that there was no time to be lost, as she was shrinking rapidly; so she set to work at once to eat some of the other bit. Her chin was pressed so closely against her foot, that there was hardly room to open her mouth; but she did it at last, and managed to swallow a morsel of the left-hand bit.

*　　*　　*　　*　　*

*　　*　　*　　*

*　　*　　*　　*　　*

"Come, my head's free at last!" said Alice in a tone of delight, which changed into alarm in another moment, when she found that her shoulders were nowhere to be found: all she could see, when she looked down, was an immense length of neck, which seemed to rise like a stalk out of a sea of green leaves that lay far below her.

"What *can* all that green stuff be?" said Alice. "And where *have* my shoulders got to? And oh, my poor hands, how is it I can't see you?" She was moving them about, as she spoke, but no result seemed to follow, except a little shaking among the distant green leaves.

As there seemed to be no chance of getting her hands up to her head, she tried to get her head down to *them*, and was delighted to find that her neck would bend about easily in any direction, like a serpent. She had just succeeded in curving it down into a graceful zigzag, and was going to dive in among the leaves, which she found to be nothing but the tops of the trees under which she had been wandering, when a sharp hiss made her draw back in a hurry: a large pigeon had flown into her face, and was beating her violently with its wings.

"Serpent!" screamed the Pigeon.

"I'm *not* a serpent!" said Alice indignantly. "Let me alone!"

"Serpent, I say again!" repeated the Pigeon, but in a more subdued tone, and added, with a kind of sob, "I've tried every way, and nothing seems to suit them!"

"I haven't the least idea what you're talking about," said Alice.

"I've tried the roots of trees, and I've tried banks, and I've tried hedges," the Pigeon went on, without attending to her; "but those serpents! There's no pleasing them!"

Alice was more and more puzzled, but she thought there was no use in saying anything more till the Pigeon had finished.

"As if it wasn't trouble enough hatching the eggs," said the Pigeon; "but I must be on the look-out for serpents night and day! Why, I haven't had a wink of sleep these three weeks!"

"I'm very sorry you've been annoyed," said Alice, who was beginning to see its meaning.

"And just as I'd taken the highest tree in the wood," continued the Pigeon, raising its voice to a shriek, "and just as I was thinking I should be free of them at last, they must needs come wriggling down from the sky! Ugh, Serpent!"

"But I'm *not* a serpent, I tell you!" said Alice. "I'm a—I'm a—"

"Well! *What* are you?" said the Pigeon. "I can see you're trying to invent something!"

"I—I'm a little girl," said Alice, rather doubtfully, as she remembered the number of changes she had gone through, that day.

"A likely story indeed!" said the Pigeon in a tone of the deepest contempt. "I've seen a good many little girls in my time, but never *one* with such a neck as that! No, no! You're a serpent; and there's no use denying it. I suppose you'll be telling me next that you never tasted an egg!"

"I *have* tasted eggs, certainly," said Alice, who was a very truthful child; "but little girls eat eggs quite as much as serpents do, you know."

"I don't believe it," said the Pigeon; "but if they do, why, then they're a kind of serpent: that's all I can say."

This was such a new idea to Alice, that she was quite silent for a minute or two, which gave the Pigeon the opportunity of adding, "You're looking for eggs, I know *that* well enough; and what does it matter to me whether you're a little girl or a serpent?"

"It matters a good deal to *me*," said Alice hastily; "but I'm not looking for eggs, as it happens; and if I was, I shouldn't want *yours*: I don't like them raw."

"Well, be off, then!" said the Pigeon in a sulky tone, as it settled down again

into its nest. Alice crouched down among the trees as well as she could, for her neck kept getting entangled among the branches, and every now and then she had to stop and untwist it. After a while she remembered that she still held the pieces of mushroom in her hands, and she set to work very carefully, nibbling first at one and then at the other, and growing sometimes taller and sometimes shorter, until she had succeeded in bringing herself down to her usual height.

It was so long since she had been anything near the right size, that it felt quite strange at first; but she got used to it in a few minutes, and began talking to herself, as usual. "Come, there's half my plan done now! How puzzling all these changes are! I'm never sure what I'm going to be, from one minute to another! However, I've got back to my right size: the next thing is, to get into that beautiful garden—how *is* that to be done, I wonder?" As she said this, she came suddenly upon an open place, with a little house in it about four feet high. "Whoever lives there," thought Alice, "it'll never do to come upon them *this* size: why, I should frighten them out of their wits!" So she began nibbling at the right-hand bit again, and did not venture to go near the house till she had brought herself down to nine inches high.

CHAPTER 6

Pig and Pepper

For a minute or two she stood looking at the house, and wondering what to do next, when suddenly a footman in livery came running out of the wood—(she considered him to be a footman because he was in livery: otherwise, judging by his face only, she would have called him a fish)—and rapped loudly at the door with his knuckles. It was opened by another footman in livery, with a round face and large eyes like a frog; and both footmen, Alice noticed, had powdered hair that curled all over their heads. She felt very curious to know what it was all about, and crept a little way out of the wood to listen.

The Fish-Footman began by producing from under his arm a great letter, nearly as large as himself, and this he handed over to the other, saying, in a solemn tone, "For the Duchess. An invitation from the Queen to play croquet." The Frog-Footman repeated, in the same solemn tone, only changing the order of the words a little, "From the Queen. An invitation for the Duchess to play croquet."

Then they both bowed low, and their curls got entangled together.

Alice laughed so much at this that she had to run back into the wood for fear of their hearing her; and when she next peeped out, the Fish-Footman was gone, and the other was sitting on the ground near the door, staring stupidly up into the sky.

Alice went timidly up to the door, and knocked.

"There's no sort of use in knocking," said the Footman, "and that for two reasons. First, because I'm on the same side of the door as you are. Secondly, because they're making such a noise inside, no one could possibly hear you." And certainly there *was* a most extraordinary noise going on within—a constant howling and sneezing, and every now and then a great crash, as if a dish or kettle had been broken to pieces.

"Please, then," said Alice, "how am I to get in?"

"There might be some sense in your knocking," the Footman went on, without attending to her, "if we had the door between us. For instance, if you were *inside*, you might knock, and I could let you out, you know." He was looking up into the sky all the time he was speaking, and this Alice thought decidedly uncivil. "But perhaps he can't help it," she said to herself; "his eyes are so *very* nearly at the top of his head. But at any rate he might answer questions.—How am I to get in?" she repeated, aloud.

"I shall sit here," the Footman remarked, "till tomorrow—"

At this moment the door of the house opened, and a large plate came skimming out, straight at the Footman's head: it just grazed his nose, and broke to pieces against one of the trees behind him.

"—or next day, maybe," the Footman continued in the same tone, exactly as if nothing had happened.

"How am I to get in?" asked Alice again, in a louder tone.

"*Are* you to get in at all?" said the Footman. "That's the first question, you know."

It was, no doubt: only Alice did not like to be told so. "It's really dreadful," she muttered to herself, "the way all the creatures argue. It's enough to drive one crazy!"

The Footman seemed to think this a good opportunity for repeating his remark, with variations. "I shall sit here," he said, "on and off, for days and days."

"But what am *I* to do?" said Alice.

"Anything you like," said the Footman, and began whistling.

"Oh, there's no use in talking to him," said Alice desperately: "he's perfectly idiotic!" And she opened the door and went in.

The door led right into a large kitchen, which was full of smoke from one end to the other: the Duchess was sitting on a three-legged stool in the middle, nursing a baby: the cook was leaning over the fire, stirring a large cauldron which seemed to be full of soup.

"There's certainly too much pepper in that soup!" Alice said to herself, as well as she could for sneezing.

There was certainly too much of it in the *air*. Even the Duchess sneezed occasionally; and as for the baby, it was sneezing and howling alternately without a moment's pause. The only things in the kitchen, that did *not* sneeze, were the cook, and a large cat, which was sitting on the hearth and grinning from ear to ear.

"Please would you tell me," said Alice, a little timidly, for she was not quite sure whether it was good manners for her to speak first, "why your cat grins like that?"

"It's a Cheshire cat," said the Duchess, "and that's why. Pig!"

She said the last word with such sudden violence that Alice quite jumped; but she saw in another moment that it was addressed to the baby, and not to her, so she took courage, and went on again:—

"I didn't know that Cheshire cats always grinned; in fact, I didn't know that cats *could* grin."

"They all can," said the Duchess; "and most of 'em do."

"I don't know of any that do," Alice said very politely, feeling quite pleased to have got into a conversation.

"You don't know much," said the Duchess; "and that's a fact."

Alice did not at all like the tone of this remark, and thought it would be as well to introduce some other subject of conversation. While she was trying to fix on one, the cook took the cauldron of soup off the fire, and at once set to work throwing everything within her reach at the Duchess and the baby —the fire-irons came first; then followed a shower of saucepans, plates, and dishes. The Duchess took no notice of them even when they hit her; and the baby was howling so much already, that it was quite impossible to say whether the blows hurt it or not.

"Oh, *please* mind what you're doing!" cried Alice, jumping up and down in an agony of terror. "Oh, there goes his *precious* nose" as an unusually large saucepan flew close by it, and very nearly carried it off.

"If everybody minded their own business," the Duchess said, in a hoarse growl,

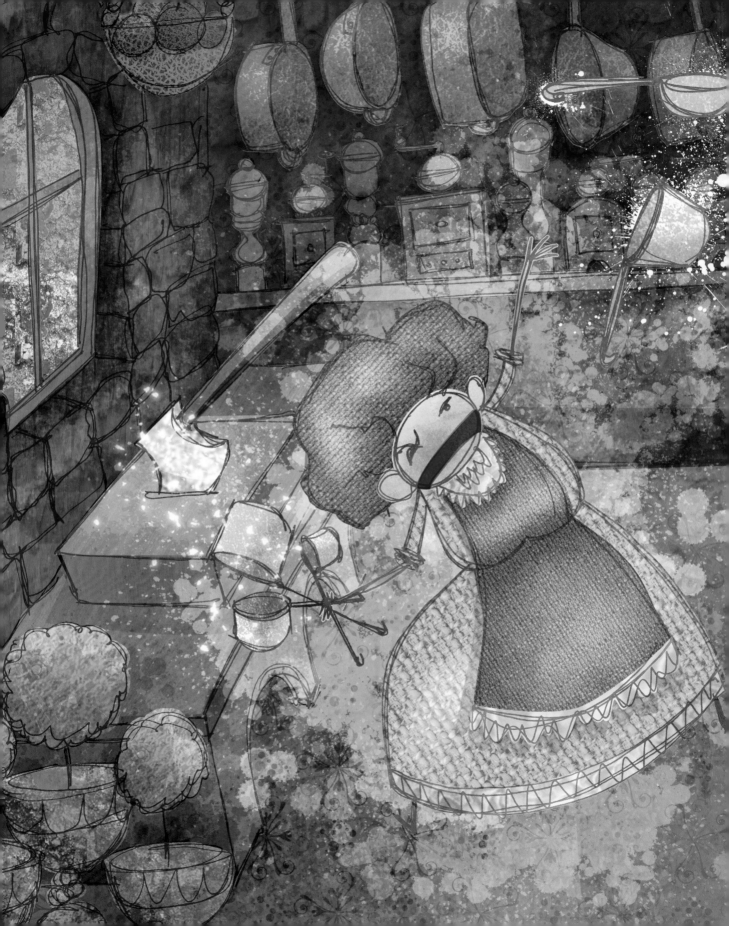

"the world would go round a deal faster than it does."

"Which would *not* be an advantage," said Alice, who felt very glad to get an opportunity of showing off a little of her knowledge. "Just think of what work it would make with the day and night! You see the earth takes twenty-four hours to turn round on its axis—"

"Talking of axes," said the Duchess, "chop off her head!"

Alice glanced rather anxiously at the cook, to see if she meant to take the hint; but the cook was busily stirring the soup, and seemed not to be listening, so she went on again: "Twenty-four hours, I *think*; or is it twelve? I—"

"Oh, don't bother *me*," said the Duchess. "I never could abide figures!" And with that she began nursing her child again, singing a sort of lullaby to it as she did so, and giving it a violent shake at the end of every line:—

> "Speak roughly to your little boy,
>   And beat him when he sneezes:
> He only does it to annoy,
>   Because he knows it teases."
> CHORUS
> (In which the cook and the baby joined):—
> "Wow! wow! wow!"

While the Duchess sang the second verse of the song, she kept tossing the baby violently up and down, and the poor little thing howled so, that Alice could hardly hear the words:—

> "I speak severely to my boy,
>   And I beat him when he sneezes:
> For he can thoroughly enjoy
>   The pepper when he pleases!"
> CHORUS
> "Wow! wow! wow!"

"Here! you may nurse it a bit, if you like!" the Duchess said to Alice, flinging the baby at her as she spoke. "I must go and get ready to play croquet with the

THE
COOK'S
Pork
& pepper
SOUP

Pork and Pepper

SOUP

This soup is easy enough that you won't feel the need to hurl all
your pots across the kitchen. It's also not overly sneezy, with a playful
array of sweet bell peppers, spicy peppers and ground black pepper.
With a little luck your kitchen won't fill up with smoke.

Makes 6 (or more, in small teacups)

Ingredients

canola or olive oil, for cooking

1 onion, peeled and chopped

1 jalapeño pepper, seeded and
finely chopped

¼ cup (60 mL) chopped fresh
cilantro (stems work well
here)

2 garlic cloves, crushed

2 tsp (10 mL) chili powder

1 tsp (5 mL) cumin

½–1 lb (250–500 g) ground pork
or spicy Italian sausage

1 red, yellow or orange bell
pepper, seeded and chopped

4 cups (1 L) beef or chicken
stock

1 cup (250 mL) salsa, or
chopped fresh or canned
diced tomatoes with their
juice

one 19 oz (540 mL) can
chickpeas, black beans or
kidney beans, drained

salt and ground black pepper

sour cream or plain yogurt,
for serving

chopped fresh cilantro,
for garnish (optional)

In a medium pot, heat a drizzle of oil over medium-high heat.
Sauté the onion for 3 to 4 minutes, until soft; add the jalapeño,
cilantro, garlic, chili powder and cumin and cook for another
2 minutes.

Add the ground pork or squeeze the Italian sausage out of its
casing into the pot. Add the bell pepper and cook, stirring and
breaking up the meat with a spoon, until it's browned and no
longer pink.

Add the stock and salsa along with the chickpeas and bring to
a simmer; cook for 20 to 30 minutes, until the vegetables are soft
and the soup has thickened slightly. Season with salt and plenty
of pepper. Serve topped with sour cream and cilantro, if you like.

Queen," and she hurried out of the room. The cook threw a frying-pan after her as she went, but it just missed her.

Alice caught the baby with some difficulty, as it was a queer-shaped little creature, and held out its arms and legs in all directions, "just like a star-fish," thought Alice. The poor little thing was snorting like a steam-engine when she caught it, and kept doubling itself up and straightening itself out again, so that altogether, for the first minute or two, it was as much as she could do to hold it.

As soon as she had made out the proper way of nursing it (which was to twist it up into a sort of knot, and then keep tight hold of its right ear and left foot, so as to prevent its undoing itself), she carried it out into the open air. "If I don't take this child away with me," thought Alice, "they're sure to kill it in a day or two. Wouldn't it be murder to leave it behind?" She said the last words out loud, and the little thing grunted in reply (it had left off sneezing by this time). "Don't grunt," said Alice; "that's not at all a proper way of expressing yourself."

The baby grunted again, and Alice looked very anxiously into its face to see what was the matter with it. There could be no doubt that it had a *very* turn-up nose, much more like a snout than a real nose: also its eyes were getting extremely small for a baby: altogether Alice did not like the look of the thing at all. "But perhaps it was only sobbing," she thought, and looked into its eyes again, to see if there were any tears.

No, there were no tears. "If you're going to turn into a pig, my dear," said Alice, seriously, "I'll have nothing more to do with you. Mind now!" The poor little thing sobbed again (or grunted, it was impossible to say which), and they went on for some while in silence.

Alice was just beginning to think to herself, "Now, what am I to do with this creature when I get it home?" when it grunted again, so violently, that she looked down into its face in some alarm. This time there could be *no* mistake about it: it was neither more nor less than a pig, and she felt that it would be quite absurd for her to carry it any further.

So she set the little creature down, and felt quite relieved to see it trot away quietly into the wood. "If it had grown up," she said to herself, "it would have made a dreadfully ugly child: but it makes rather a handsome pig, I think." And she began thinking over other children she knew, who might do very well as pigs, and

was just saying to herself, "if one only knew the right way to change them—" when she was a little startled by seeing the Cheshire Cat sitting on a bough of a tree a few yards off.

The Cat only grinned when it saw Alice. It looked good-natured, she thought: still it had *very* long claws and a great many teeth, so she felt that it ought to be treated with respect.

"Cheshire Puss," she began, rather timidly, as she did not at all know whether it would like the name: however, it only grinned a little wider. "Come, it's pleased so far," thought Alice, and she went on. "Would you tell me, please, which way I ought to go from here?"

"That depends a good deal on where you want to get to," said the Cat.

"I don't much care where—" said Alice.

"Then it doesn't matter which way you go," said the Cat.

"—so long as I get *somewhere*," Alice added as an explanation.

"Oh, you're sure to do that," said the Cat, "if you only walk long enough."

Alice felt that this could not be denied, so she tried another question. "What sort of people live about here?"

"In *that* direction," the Cat said, waving its right paw round, "lives a Hatter: and in *that* direction," waving the other paw, "lives a March Hare. Visit either you like: they're both mad."

"But I don't want to go among mad people," Alice remarked.

"Oh, you can't help that," said the Cat: "we're all mad here. I'm mad. You're mad."

"How do you know I'm mad?" said Alice.

"You must be," said the Cat, "or you wouldn't have come here."

Alice didn't think that proved it at all; however, she went on: "And how do you know that you're mad?"

"To begin with," said the Cat, "a dog's not mad. You grant that?"

"I suppose so," said Alice.

"Well, then," the Cat went on, "you see a dog growls when it's angry, and wags its tail when it's pleased. Now *I* growl when I'm pleased, and wag my tail when I'm angry. Therefore I'm mad."

"*I* call it purring, not growling," said Alice.

"Call it what you like," said the Cat. "Do you play croquet with the Queen to-day?"

"I should like it very much," said Alice, "but I haven't been invited yet."

"You'll see me there," said the Cat, and vanished.

Alice was not much surprised at this, she was getting so well used to queer things happening. While she was still looking at the place where it had been, it suddenly appeared again.

"By-the-bye, what became of the baby?" said the Cat. "I'd nearly forgotten to ask."

"It turned into a pig," Alice answered very quietly, just as if the Cat had come back in a natural way.

"I thought it would," said the Cat, and vanished again.

Alice waited a little, half expecting to see it again, but it did not appear, and after a minute or two she walked on in the direction in which the March Hare was said to live. "I've seen hatters before," she said to herself: "the March Hare will be much the most interesting, and perhaps, as this is May, it won't be raving mad—at least not so mad as it was in March." As she said this, she looked up, and there was the Cat again, sitting on a branch of a tree.

"Did you say 'pig', or 'fig'?" said the Cat.

"I said 'pig'," replied Alice; "and I wish you wouldn't keep appearing and vanishing so suddenly: you make one quite giddy."

"All right," said the Cat; and this time it vanished quite slowly, beginning with the end of the tail, and ending with the grin, which remained some time after the rest of it had gone.

"Well! I've often seen a cat without a grin," thought Alice; "but a grin without a cat! It's the most curious thing I ever saw in my life!"

She had not gone much farther before she came in sight of the house of the March Hare: she thought it must be the right house, because the chimneys were shaped like ears and the roof was thatched with fur. It was so large a house, that she did not like to go nearer till she had nibbled some more of the left-hand bit of mushroom, and raised herself to about two feet high: even then she walked up towards it rather timidly, saying to herself "Suppose it should be raving mad after all! I almost wish I'd gone to see the Hatter instead!"

CHESHIRE CAT'S

Trinny

GRAINY MUSTARD

rarebit

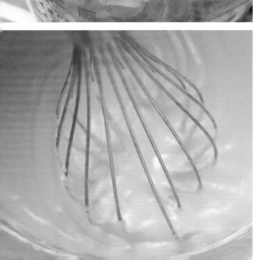

Grinny Grainy Mustard Rarebit

Well! If you happen to see a cat with a grin, or a grin with a cat,
you can be sure that cat has just eaten grainy mustard, which makes
all cats quite giddy—and that's a fact, in case you didn't know.

Provides 4 cheesy Cheshire grins

Ingredients

2 Tbsp (30 mL) butter, plus extra for buttering

2 Tbsp (30 mL) flour

1 cup (250 mL) beer or milk

2 cups (500 mL) grated aged cheddar or Gouda cheese

1 Tbsp (15 mL) grainy mustard

salt and ground black pepper

4 thick slices good-quality crusty bread

Alice's advice

Cats love to get their paws on canapés. If you want daintier, two-bite sandwiches for your tea party, toast thin slices of baguette and top with cheese sauce; serve straight up or place under the broiler for a minute or two, until bubbly and golden.

In a medium saucepan, heat the butter and flour over medium-high heat until the butter melts; whisk until smooth, then whisk in the beer or milk and bring to a boil. Once the mixture bubbles, cook it for a full minute, stirring until it thickens, then turn the heat down to low and stir in the cheese and mustard. Season with salt and pepper and whisk until melted and smooth.

Toast the bread in the toaster, if it will accommodate thick slices, or on a baking sheet in a 400°F (200°C) oven until golden. Butter the toast, if you like. Pour the cheese sauce overtop and serve as is, or place the cheese-topped slices on a baking sheet and put under the broiler for 2 minutes, until bubbly and golden.

CHAPTER 7

A Mad Tea-Party

There was a table set out under a tree in front of the house, and the March Hare and the Hatter were having tea at it: a Dormouse was sitting between them, fast asleep, and the other two were using it as a cushion, resting their elbows on it, and talking over its head. "Very uncomfortable for the Dormouse," thought Alice; "only, as it's asleep, I suppose it doesn't mind."

The table was a large one, but the three were all crowded together at one corner of it. "No room! No room!" they cried out when they saw Alice coming.

"There's *plenty* of room!" said Alice indignantly, and she sat down in a large arm-chair at one end of the table.

"Have some wine," the March Hare said in an encouraging tone.

Alice looked all round the table, but there was nothing on it but tea. "I don't see any wine," she remarked.

"There isn't any," said the March Hare.

"Then it wasn't very civil of you to offer it," said Alice angrily.

"It wasn't very civil of you to sit down without being invited," said the March Hare.

"I didn't know it was *your* table," said Alice; "it's laid for a great many more than three."

"Your hair wants cutting," said the Hatter. He had been looking at Alice for some time with great curiosity, and this was his first speech.

"You should learn not to make personal remarks," Alice said with some severity: "it's very rude."

The Hatter opened his eyes very wide on hearing this; but all he *said* was, "Why is a raven like a writing-desk?"

"Come, we shall have some fun now!" thought Alice. "I'm glad they've begun asking riddles.—I believe I can guess that," she added aloud.

"Do you mean that you think you can find out the answer to it?" said the March Hare.

"Exactly so," said Alice.

"Then you should say what you mean," the March Hare went on.

"I do," Alice hastily replied; "at least—at least I mean what I say—that's the same thing, you know."

"Not the same thing a bit!" said the Hatter. "Why, you might just as well say that 'I see what I eat' is the same thing as 'I eat what I see'!"

"You might just as well say," added the March Hare, "that 'I like what I get' is the same thing as 'I get what I like'!"

"You might just as well say," added the Dormouse, who seemed to be talking in its sleep, "that 'I breathe when I sleep' is the same thing as 'I sleep when I breathe'!"

"It *is* the same thing with you," said the Hatter, and here the conversation dropped, and the party sat silent for a minute, while Alice thought over all she could remember about ravens and writing-desks, which wasn't much.

The Hatter was the first to break the silence. "What day of the month is it?" he said, turning to Alice: he had taken his watch out of his pocket, and was looking at it uneasily, shaking it every now and then, and holding it to his ear.

Alice considered a little, and then said, "The fourth."

"Two days wrong!" sighed the Hatter. "I told you butter wouldn't suit the works!" he added, looking angrily at the March Hare.

"It was the *best* butter," the March Hare meekly replied.

"Yes, but some crumbs must have got in as well," the Hatter grumbled: "you shouldn't have put it in with the bread-knife."

The March Hare took the watch and looked at it gloomily: then he dipped it into his cup of tea, and looked at it again: but he could think of nothing better to say than his first remark, "It was the *best* butter, you know."

Alice had been looking over his shoulder with some curiosity. "What a funny watch!" she remarked. "It tells the day of the month, and doesn't tell what o'clock it is!"

"Why should it?" muttered the Hatter. "Does *your* watch tell you what year it is?"

"Of course not," Alice replied very readily: "but that's because it stays the same year for such a long time together."

"Which is just the case with *mine*," said the Hatter.

Alice felt dreadfully puzzled. The Hatter's remark seemed to have no sort of meaning in it, and yet it was certainly English. "I don't quite understand you," she said, as politely as she could.

"The Dormouse is asleep again," said the Hatter, and he poured a little hot tea upon its nose.

The Dormouse shook its head impatiently, and said, without opening its eyes, "Of course, of course; just what I was going to remark myself."

"Have you guessed the riddle yet?" the Hatter said, turning to Alice again.

"No, I give it up," Alice replied. "What's the answer?"

"I haven't the slightest idea," said the Hatter.

"Nor I," said the March Hare.

Alice sighed wearily. "I think you might do something better with the time," she said, "than wasting it in asking riddles that have no answers."

"If you knew Time as well as I do," said the Hatter, "you wouldn't talk about wasting *it*. It's *him*."

"I don't know what you mean," said Alice.

"Of course you don't!" the Hatter said, tossing his head contemptuously. "I dare say you never even spoke to Time!"

"Perhaps not," Alice cautiously replied; "but I know I have to beat time when I learn music."

"Ah! That accounts for it," said the Hatter. "He won't stand beating. Now, if you only kept on good terms with him, he'd do almost anything you liked with the clock. For instance, suppose it were nine o'clock in the morning, just time to begin lessons: you'd only have to whisper a hint to Time, and round goes the clock in a twinkling! Half-past one, time for dinner!"

("I only wish it was," the March Hare said to itself in a whisper.)

"That would be grand, certainly," said Alice thoughtfully: "but then—I shouldn't be hungry for it, you know."

"Not at first, perhaps," said the Hatter: "but you could keep it to half-past one as long as you liked."

"Is that the way *you* manage?" Alice asked.

The Hatter shook his head mournfully. "Not I!" he replied. "We quarrelled last March—just before *he* went mad, you know—" (pointing with his tea spoon at the March Hare), "—it was at the great concert given by the Queen of Hearts, and I had to sing.—

'Twinkle, twinkle, little bat!
How I wonder what you're at!'

"You know the song, perhaps?"

"I've heard something like it," said Alice.

"It goes on, you know," the Hatter continued, "in this way:—

'Up above the world you fly,
Like a tea-tray in the sky.
Twinkle, twinkle—'"

Here the Dormouse shook itself, and began singing in its sleep "Twinkle, twinkle, twinkle, twinkle—" and went on so long that they had to pinch it to make it stop.

"Well, I'd hardly finished the first verse," said the Hatter, "when the Queen bawled out, 'He's murdering the time! Off with his head!'"

"How dreadfully savage!" exclaimed Alice.

"And ever since that," the Hatter went on in a mournful tone, "he won't do a thing I ask! It's always six o'clock now."

A bright idea came into Alice's head. "Is that the reason so many tea-things are put out here?" she asked.

"Yes, that's it," said the Hatter with a sigh: "it's always tea-time, and we've no time to wash the things between whiles."

"Then you keep moving round, I suppose?" said Alice.

"Exactly so," said the Hatter: "as the things get used up."

"But what happens when you come to the beginning again?" Alice ventured to ask.

"Suppose we change the subject," the March Hare interrupted, yawning. "I'm getting tired of this. I vote the young lady tells us a story."

"I'm afraid I don't know one," said Alice, rather alarmed at the proposal.

"Then the Dormouse shall!" they both cried. "Wake up, Dormouse!" And they pinched it on both sides at once.

The Dormouse slowly opened his eyes. "I wasn't asleep," it said in a hoarse, feeble voice, "I heard every word you fellows were saying."

"Tell us a story!" said the March Hare.

"Yes, please do!" pleaded Alice.

"And be quick about it," added the Hatter, "or you'll be asleep again before it's done."

"Once upon a time there were three little sisters," the Dormouse began in a great hurry; "and their names were Elsie, Lacie, and Tillie; and they lived at the bottom of a well—"

"What did they live on?" said Alice, who always took a great interest in questions of eating and drinking.

"They lived on treacle," said the Dormouse, after thinking a minute or two.

"They couldn't have done that, you know," Alice gently remarked. "They'd have been ill."

"So they were," said the Dormouse; "*very* ill."

Alice tried to fancy to herself what such an extraordinary way of living would be like, but it puzzled her too much: so she went on: "But why did they live at the bottom of a well?"

"Take some more tea," the March Hare said to Alice, very earnestly.

"I've had nothing yet," Alice replied in an offended tone, "so I can't take more."

"You mean you can't take *less*," said the Hatter: "it's very easy to take *more* than nothing."

"Nobody asked *your* opinion," said Alice.

"Who's making personal remarks now?" the Hatter asked triumphantly.

Alice did not quite know what to say to this: so she helped herself to some tea and bread-and-butter, and then turned to the Dormouse, and repeated her question. "Why did they live at the bottom of a well?"

The Dormouse again took a minute or two to think about it, and then said, "It was a treacle-well."

"There's no such thing!" Alice was beginning very angrily, but the Hatter and the March Hare went "Sh! Sh!" and the Dormouse sulkily remarked, "If you can't be civil, you'd better finish the story for yourself."

"No, please go on!" Alice said very humbly. "I won't interrupt again. I dare say there may be *one*."

"One, indeed!" said the Dormouse indignantly. However, he consented to go on. "And so these three little sisters—they were learning to draw, you know—"

"What did they draw?" said Alice, quite forgetting her promise.

"Treacle," said the Dormouse, without considering at all this time.

"I want a clean cup," interrupted the Hatter: "let's all move one place on."

He moved on as he spoke, and the Dormouse followed him: the March Hare moved into the Dormouse's place, and Alice rather unwillingly took the place of the March Hare. The Hatter was the only one who got any advantage from the change; and Alice was a good deal worse off than before, as the March Hare had just upset the milk-jug into his plate.

Alice did not wish to offend the Dormouse again, so she began very cautiously: "But I don't understand. Where did they draw the treacle from?"

"You can draw water out of a water-well," said the Hatter; "so I should think you could draw treacle out of a treacle-well—eh, stupid?"

"But they were *in* the well," Alice said to the Dormouse, not choosing to notice this last remark.

"Of course they were," said the Dormouse; "well in."

This answer so confused poor Alice, that she let the Dormouse go on for some time without interrupting it.

"They were learning to draw," the Dormouse went on, yawning and rubbing its eyes, for it was getting very sleepy; "and they drew all manner of things— everything that begins with an M—"

"Why with an M?" said Alice.

"Why not?" said the March Hare.

Alice was silent.

The Dormouse had closed its eyes by this time, and was going off into a doze; but, on being pinched by the Hatter, it woke up again with a little shriek, and went on: "—that begins with an M, such as mouse-traps, and the moon, and memory, and muchness— you know you say things are 'much of a muchness'—did you ever see such a thing as a drawing of a muchness?"

"Really, now you ask me," said Alice, very much confused, "I don't think—"

"Then you shouldn't talk," said the Hatter.

This piece of rudeness was more than Alice could bear: she got up in great disgust, and walked off: the Dormouse fell asleep instantly, and neither of the others took the least notice of her going, though she looked back once or twice, half hoping that they would call after her: the last time she saw them, they were trying to put the Dormouse into the teapot.

"At any rate I'll never go *there* again!" said Alice as she picked her way through the wood. "It's the stupidest tea-party I ever was at in all my life!"

Just as she said this, she noticed that one of the trees had a door leading right into it. "That's very curious!" she thought. "But everything's curious to-day. I think I may as well go in at once." And in she went.

Once more she found herself in the long hall, and close to the little glass table. "Now, I'll manage better this time," she said to herself, and began by taking the little golden key, and unlocking the door that led into the garden. Then she set to work nibbling at the mushroom (she had kept a piece of it in her pocket) till she was about a foot high: then she walked down the little passage: and *then*—she found herself at last in the beautiful garden, among the bright flower-beds and the cool fountains.

THE MAD HATTER'S Tea party

In Wonderland the tea party never ends. Ever.
Taste the tantalizing tea-time treats from the three-tiered
tea tower with this capital tea.

The precocious Alice, the jittery March Hare, the dormant Dormouse
and the mad-capped Mad Hatter offer their own versions
of a scone, a savoury, a sweet and a unique tea concoction.

We're all mad here. I'm mad. You're mad.
But that doesn't mean we can't be civil and have a proper cup of tea.

Dormouse

TEA Sleepy Warm-Milk Tea

SCONE Curled-Up Treacle Scones

SAVOURY Sleepy Turkey Roll-Ups

SWEET Sticky Toffee Teacakes
with Treacle Frosting

*Tea for Two, Two for Tea . . .
Brew a Proper Pot of Tea*

March Hare

TEA Milky Mystic Matcha

SCONE Carrot Scones with
Cream-Cheese Schmear

SAVOURY Ginger-Carrot
Sandwiches

SWEET Best Butter Shortbread

Tea Sandwiches: A Visual Guide

Mad Hatter

TEA Crazy-8 Iced Tea

SCONE No-Time Cream
Drop-Scones

SAVOURY Stack-of-Cards
Club Sandwich

SWEET Sunken Dark-Chocolate
Cake with Raspberry Fool

Tasseography: Reading Tea Leaves

Alice

TEA Fizzy Iced Tea

SCONE Oat and Currant Scones
with Lemon Curd

SAVOURY Little Girl Bacon-and-
Egg-Salad Sandwiches

SWEET No-Wine Jellies

Sleepy Warm-Milk Tea

If you're having trouble making Zs, start with some Ms—warm Milk will
help escort you peacefully and deliciously to sleep. Mmmmm . . .

Serves 2 snuggle buddies

Ingredients

1 Tbsp (15 mL) loose herbal
or chamomile tea leaves
(or 2 tea bags)

¼–½ cup (60–125 mL)
sweetened condensed milk

sugar or honey to taste

Place the tea leaves (or tea bags) in a teapot, in a tea ball or stick
if necessary. Pour about 2 cups (500 mL) of boiling water over the
tea, cover and let steep for about 5 minutes. If you are using tea
leaves, use a tea strainer to strain the leaves while pouring. Pour
the tea into 2 mugs. Stir in as much of the sweetened condensed
milk as desired, and add the sugar to taste, if needed. Serve warm.

DORMOUSE'S

Curled-Up Treacle Scones

Sweet, home sweet. Living at the bottom of a treacle well
makes it easy to be drawn into curling up and laying down
to a nice treacle nap on a soft scone pillow.

Makes 9 warm, curled-up scones

Ingredients

STICKINESS

2 Tbsp (30 mL) butter

¼ cup (60 mL) packed brown
sugar

1 Tbsp (15 mL) golden syrup,
fancy molasses or treacle

DOUGH

2 cups (500 mL) all-purpose
flour

1 Tbsp (15 mL) baking powder

1 Tbsp (15 mL) sugar

¼ tsp (1 mL) salt

¾ cup (185 mL) milk

¼ cup (60 mL) canola or other
mild vegetable oil

FILLING

½ cup (125 mL) packed brown
sugar

2 Tbsp (30 mL) golden syrup,
fancy molasses or treacle

½ tsp (2 mL) cinnamon

¼ cup (60 mL) chopped pecans
(optional)

TO MAKE THE STICKINESS Put the butter, brown sugar and syrup
into a greased 8-inch (20 cm) square pan. To melt, put it in the
oven and turn the oven on to 350°F (180°C).

TO MAKE THE DOUGH In a large bowl, stir together the flour,
baking powder, sugar and salt. Add the milk and oil and stir by
hand just until you have a soft dough. On a lightly floured surface,
pat or roll the dough into a 9- × 14-inch (23 × 35 cm) rectangle.

TO MAKE THE FILLING Sprinkle the dough evenly with the brown
sugar, drizzle evenly with the syrup and sprinkle evenly with the
cinnamon and pecans (if using).

Starting from a long side, roll the dough into a jelly-roll-style log.
Using a serrated knife (dental floss or heavy thread can also be
used), cut the roll into 9 biscuits.

Remove the pan from the oven and stir the melted stickiness
to combine. Place the biscuits cut-side down in 3 rows of 3 on the
stickiness in the pan.

Bake for 20 minutes, until golden and bubbly. Invert onto a
platter while still warm.

Sleepy Turkey Roll-Ups

Wrap and roll up in a big, cozy blanket and tuck into a naptime snack
with these snuggly turkey rolls. Or slice and serve them to your friends
for tea, and be the life of the party.

Serves 8 to 16 cozy critters

Ingredients

- 1 pkg (8 oz/250 g) spreadable cream cheese, at room temperature
- 1 pkg (4 oz/120 g) soft goat's cheese
- ¼ lb (250 g) sliced turkey, chopped, or 1 cup (250 mL) chopped roasted turkey or chicken
- ½ cup (125 mL) pecans, toasted and finely chopped
- ¼ cup (60 mL) dried cranberries, chopped
- ¼ cup (60 mL) chopped fresh parsley
- salt and ground black pepper to taste
- 4–6 large or 8 small flour tortillas, regular or whole wheat
- spring greens or pea shoots (optional)

In a medium bowl, beat the cream cheese and goat's cheese until well blended and smooth. Stir in the turkey, pecans, cranberries and parsley; season with salt and pepper.

Spread each tortilla with the mixture. Top with a few greens, if you like. Tightly roll up each tortilla and cut into ¾-inch (2 cm) slices on a slight diagonal to serve for tea.

Sticky Toffee Teacakes

WITH TREACLE FROSTING

"Sweet, sticky treacle treats to eat with tea."
Say it three times fast, with your mouth full . . .

Makes 1 dozen cupcakes or 2 dozen mini cupcakes

Ingredients

TEACAKES

1 cup (250 mL) dried dates, golden raisins and chopped dried apricots

¼ cup (60 mL) butter, at room temperature

¼ cup (60 mL) canola oil

1 cup (250 mL) packed brown sugar

2 large eggs

2 Tbsp (30 mL) golden syrup, fancy molasses or treacle

1 tsp (5 mL) vanilla

2 cups (500 mL) all-purpose flour

2 tsp (10 mL) baking powder

½ tsp (2 mL) cinnamon

¼ tsp (1 mL) salt

TREACLE FROSTING

1 pkg (8 oz/250 g) cream cheese, at room temperature

¼ cup (60 mL) butter, at room temperature

3 cups (750 mL) icing sugar

2 Tbsp (30 mL) golden syrup, fancy molasses or treacle

1 Tbsp (15 mL) milk, half and half, 18% cream or water

½ tsp (2 mL) vanilla

Preheat the oven to 350°F (180°C) and line 12 muffin tins (or 24 mini muffin tins) with paper liners.

TO MAKE THE TEACAKES Put the dates, raisins and apricots into a heatproof bowl and pour 1 cup (250 mL) boiling water overtop. Let stand for 15 minutes, until soft. Mash it well with a fork or pour into a food processor and pulse until well blended but still a bit chunky.

Meanwhile, in a large bowl, beat the butter, oil and brown sugar with an electric mixer for a few minutes, until well blended and light. Add the eggs, syrup and vanilla and beat well.

In a small bowl, stir together the flour, baking powder, cinnamon and salt. Add about a third of the flour mixture to the butter mixture, stirring or beating on low speed just until incorporated. Add half the puréed fruit in the same manner, then another third of the flour, then the rest of the puréed fruit and the rest of the flour, mixing just until blended.

Divide the batter among the prepared muffin tins and bake for 25 to 30 minutes (for regular-sized cupcakes) or 20 to 25 minutes (for mini cupcakes), until golden and the tops are domed and springy to the touch. Tip them slightly in their tins to allow steam to escape and help them cool completely.

TO MAKE THE TREACLE FROSTING In a large bowl, beat the cream cheese and butter for a few minutes, until smooth and fluffy. Gradually beat in the icing sugar, syrup, milk and vanilla until you have a soft, spreadable consistency, adding a little extra sugar or liquid if you need it. Frost the cupcakes once they have cooled completely.

Tea for Two, Two for Tea...

BREW A PROPER POT OF TEA

Some say tea time is three in the afternoon, some say four in the mid-afternoon and some say five in the evening. But no matter what people say, it is always tea time somewhere in the world. So brew a cup and get your pinkies up.

step #1

Fill a kettle with cold water. (Do not draw the water from a well; if it turns out to be a treacle well, you will find yourself in a sticky predicament.) Bring the kettle to a boil.

step #2

In the meantime, fill your teapot with hot water from the tap and let the pot warm up to the idea of having boiling water in it.

step #3

Also in the meantime, prepare a tea tray. Assemble your cups and saucers and arrange them on a silver tea tray. Fill a small jug with cold milk and a small bowl with sugar—lumps or otherwise. Cuddle them cozily together on the tea tray. Pile up a plate with assorted tea biscuits and other small treats. You can sneak a treat now if no one is watching.

step #4

Choose tea bags or loose tea leaves (or use tea bags you've made yourself and filled with loose tea leaves). Pour the warm water out of the teapot. Add 1 heaping teaspoon (5 mL) of black tea for each cup. Pour the boiling water into the pot so the leaves kick up and swirl about like a snow globe. Let the tea steep for 3 to 5 minutes.

step #5

Allow each person to personalize their milk and sugar in a teacup. If you used loose tea leaves, you will benefit from using a small tea strainer to catch the twiggy bits before they get in your cup.

step #6

Stir your tea using a little silver spoon, never clanging the sides of the cup or spilling over the sides. Hold the handle between two fingers and your thumb and keep the cup steady. Extend your pinky for balance. Sip, don't slurp.

March Hare

Milky Mystic Matcha

Transcend time with the mystical, magical properties of a very untraditional milky matcha (green tea) latte. It will help you focus and concentrate on the present so you won't waste your time fiddling with answerless riddles.

Serves 2 bunny buddies

Ingredients

2 tsp (10 mL) powdered matcha (green tea)

½ cup (125 mL) very hot (not boiling) water

2 cups (500 mL) milk, warmed

honey, sugar or maple syrup to taste

Alice's advice

Matcha contains caffeine, so if you have kids at your tea party, you might want to substitute warm milk and honey. Or serve herbal iced tea instead.

In a small bowl or glass measuring cup, whisk the matcha into the hot water until smooth.

Whisk in the milk and honey, and froth it up with your whisk (or one of those battery-powered milk frothers). Serve warm.

Carrot Scones

Carrots will tease any hare into a tizzy. To smooth out and unfrazzle
your hare, simply use liberal amounts of cream cheese.

Makes 8 large or 16 small scones

Ingredients

CARROT SCONES

2½ cups (625 mL) all-purpose
flour

2 Tbsp (30 mL) brown sugar

1 Tbsp (15 mL) baking powder

½ tsp (2 mL) cinnamon

¼ tsp (1 mL) salt

½ cup (125 mL) butter, chilled
and cut into bits

1 large carrot, coarsely grated
(about 1 cup/250 mL)

¾ cup (185 mL) milk, half and
half or 18% cream

1 large egg

½ cup (125 mL) chopped
walnuts, pecans or raisins

CREAM-CHEESE SCHMEAR

1 pkg (8 oz/250 g) cream
cheese

2-4 Tbsp (30-40 mL) milk, half
and half or 18% cream

1 Tbsp (15 mL) honey

¼ tsp (1 mL) vanilla

Preheat the oven to 400°F (200°C).

TO MAKE THE CARROT SCONES In a bowl, stir together the flour,
brown sugar, baking powder, cinnamon and salt. Add the butter
and blend with a fork or pastry blender (or pulse the mixture in
the bowl of a food processor) until almost blended, with pieces of
butter the size of a pea remaining. Add the grated carrots and toss
to combine.

In a small bowl, stir together the milk and egg; add to the
carrot mixture along with the chopped walnuts or raisins and stir
just until the dough comes together.

On a parchment-lined baking sheet, pat the dough into a circle
about 1 inch (2.5 cm) thick. (For smaller scones, divide the dough
in half and pat into two circles.) Cut into 8 wedges with a sharp
knife, and pull the scones apart from each other, leaving 1 inch
(2.5 cm) or so between them.

Bake for 20 minutes, or until golden.

TO MAKE THE CREAM-CHEESE SCHMEAR In a bowl, beat the
cream cheese, milk, honey and vanilla with an electric mixer until
the mixture is smooth, fluffy and spreadable.

Serve the scones with the schmear alongside.

Ginger-Carrot Sandwiches

The March Hare gets around underground by rooting out carrots.
He sometimes finds himself in faraway tunnels where he simply goes
mad for all the exotic roots—like ginger. Fancy them both in a sandwich?

Makes 16 finger sandwiches

Ingredients

canola or olive oil, for cooking

2 green onions, finely chopped

½ jalapeño pepper, seeded and
  finely chopped (optional)

1 Tbsp (15 mL) grated fresh
  ginger

1 garlic clove, crushed

1 cup (250 mL) grated carrots

1 small tomato, chopped

1 tsp (5 mL) curry powder
  or paste

salt to taste

¼ cup (60 mL) chopped fresh
  cilantro

½ pkg (4 oz/125 g) cream
  cheese, at room temperature

¼ cup (60 mL) tahini (sesame
  seed paste) or peanut butter

8 slices sandwich bread, toasted
  if you like

In a heavy skillet, heat a drizzle of oil over medium-high heat.
Add the onions, jalapeño (if using), ginger and garlic and cook for
3 to 4 minutes, until soft. Add the carrots, tomato and curry
powder and cook for 3 to 4 minutes longer, until the vegetables
are just getting soft and the extra moisture has cooked off. Season
with salt and stir in the cilantro; set aside.

Spread half the slices of bread with the cream cheese and the
rest with the tahini. Top the cream cheese slices with some of the
carrot mixture, spreading it to the edges. Place the tahini slices
overtop. Trim the crusts (if you wish) and cut the sandwiches into
quarters, squares or fingers.

Best Butter Shortbread

Butter will make anything and everything better, but you really must use the best butter, you know. And there musn't be any crumbs.

Makes about 16 buttery shortbread wedges

Ingredients

½ cup (125 mL) butter, at room temperature

¼ cup (60 mL) sugar

1 tsp (5 mL) vanilla

pinch salt

¾ cup (185 mL) all-purpose flour

2 Tbsp (30 mL) cornstarch

Alice's advice

To make London Fog shortbread, add 2 tsp (10 mL) good-quality loose leaf Earl Grey tea to your dry ingredients.

Preheat the oven to 350°F (180°C).

In a medium bowl, beat the butter and sugar with an electric mixer for a minute or two, until light and creamy. Beat in the vanilla and salt.

Add the flour and cornstarch and blend on low speed, just until the dough comes together.

Pat the dough into a 9-inch (23 cm) round cake pan. Poke the surface a few times with a fork, and if you like, press down all around on the edge of the dough with the tines of the fork.

Bake for 20 minutes, or until pale golden around the edges. Cut the shortbread into wedges while it's still warm, and let the pieces cool somewhat in the pan before taking them out so that they don't crumble.

Tea Sandwiches

A VISUAL GUIDE

Finger sandwiches are like butterflies. They come in a magnificent variety of shapes and colours, and they contain quite a bit of butter. But only the best butter. Hold your tea sandwich daintily between finger and thumb, and gobble it down with great delight before it gets away!

Open-faced

Traditional

Double-decker

Triple-decker

Window frames

Pinwheel

Cucumber slice

Envelope

Square

Triangle

Little pickle on top

Big pickle on top

Edible flower
petal side dip

Chive tie

Edible
flower on top

Herby
side dip

Tomato
on top

Cherry on top

Olive on top

Microgreens
on top

Crazy-8 Iced Tea

If you have gone and quarrelled with someone, you must make up for lost time by brewing a large batch of iced tea to mend time. It's better to make extra tea because you can always take more tea, but you can't take less.

Serves 8, more or less

Ingredients

8 tea bags

8 Tbsp (125 mL) sugar or honey

8 lemon slices

lots of ice

In a medium pot, bring 8 cups (2 L) of water to a boil. Remove from the heat, add the tea bags, cover and let steep for 5 minutes. Remove the tea bags and add the sugar, stirring until completely dissolved.

Cool, then add the lemon slices and refrigerate until well chilled. Serve in tall glasses filled with ice.

No-Time Cream Drop-Scones

If you only keep on good terms with Father Time, he'll do almost anything you like with the clock. For instance, suppose you want to eat scones—you can use this time-saving recipe and enjoy freshly baked scones at the drop of a hat! Time for tea!

Makes about 1 dozen scones

Ingredients

1⅓ cups (310 mL) all-purpose flour

2 Tbsp (30 mL) sugar

1½ tsp (7 mL) baking powder

¼ tsp (1 mL) salt

1 cup (250 mL) heavy (whipping) cream

coarse sugar, for sprinkling (optional)

Alice's advice

These scones sound (and taste) rich, but are actually lighter than those made with butter. They're the fastest, easiest scones you'll ever make from scratch, and can be gussied up with lemon or orange zest, currants or raisins, fresh or frozen berries or chopped chocolate.

Preheat the oven to 400°F (200°C).

In a medium bowl, stir together the flour, sugar, baking powder and salt. Add the cream and stir just until the dough comes together.

Drop by large spoonfuls (or use a small ice-cream scoop for more uniform scones) onto a greased or parchment-lined baking sheet. If you like, sprinkle with coarse sugar.

Bake for 15 to 20 minutes, or until golden. Serve warm.

Stack-of-Cards Club Sandwich

Club sandwiches are perfectly handy for eating while playing cards
at a timeless tea time with your fellow cards. Stack the deck in
your favour and perhaps you will get the upper hand on the other
card-carrying members of the Club-Sandwich Club.

Serves 2 to 4, though four-of-a-kind beats a pair

Ingredients

6 slices sandwich bread, toasted

¼ cup (60 mL) mayonnaise, or
to taste

¼ lb (125 g) deli roast chicken
or turkey

1 ripe avocado, pitted and sliced

8 slices bacon, cooked until
crisp

salt and ground black pepper

1 ripe tomato, thinly sliced

4 green-leaf lettuce leaves, torn
to size

Lay 4 slices of toast on a cutting board, and spread each with
mayonnaise. Divide the turkey between each slice, then layer on
the avocado and bacon. Sprinkle with salt and pepper. Top with
the tomato slices and lettuce.

Stack one open-faced sandwich on top of another, and top it off
with a third piece of toast, as a lid. Cut into quarters, and help
each quarter stay stacked with a fancy toothpick.

Sunken Dark-Chocolate Cake

WITH RASPBERRY FOOL

The heart is always making the head into a fool, so
follow your heart and rush into this lovely fool.

Serves 8 to 12 fools and/or geniuses

Ingredients

CAKE

8 oz (250 g) semisweet or
  bittersweet chocolate,
  coarsely chopped

½ cup (125 mL) butter, cut
  into chunks

6 large eggs

1 cup (250 mL) sugar, divided

RASPBERRY FOOL

2 cups (500 mL) fresh or frozen
  (thawed) raspberries or
  blackberries

¼ cup (60 mL) sugar, divided

1½ cups (375 mL) heavy
  (whipping) cream

Preheat the oven to 350°F (180°C). Line the bottom of a 9-inch (23 cm) springform pan with waxed or parchment paper. Don't grease the pan—the batter needs to cling to the sides as it rises.

TO MAKE THE CAKE Gently melt the chocolate with the butter over low heat on the stovetop, or in a glass or stainless steel bowl set over a pot of simmering water. Remove from the heat and set aside to cool slightly.

Separate 4 of the eggs, putting the yolks and whites in separate medium bowls. Add the remaining 2 eggs and ½ cup (125 mL) of the sugar to the egg yolks. Whisk in the warm chocolate mixture and stir until smooth.

Beat the egg whites with an electric mixer until foamy.

Gradually add the remaining sugar, beating until the egg whites form soft mounds but aren't yet stiff. Fold about one-quarter of the egg whites into the chocolate mixture to lighten it, and then gently fold in the rest, without deflating the egg whites. Pour the batter into the prepared pan and smooth the top.

Bake for 35 to 40 minutes, until the cake is puffy and cracked on top, and the middle isn't wobbly. Cool the cake completely in the pan without loosening the sides (the batter will cling to the pan as it cools, sinking in the middle and keeping its high sides).

TO MAKE THE RASPERRY FOOL Meanwhile, in a medium bowl, gently crush the berries with half the sugar—a potato masher or whisk works well. Set aside to macerate for 10 minutes or so.

When you're ready to serve the cake, whip the cream with the rest of the sugar until softly stiff, and fold in the fruit mixture, leaving it swirled through the cream rather than blended in.

Run a thin knife around the edge of the pan to loosen the sunken cake and remove the sides of the pan. Transfer the cake to a serving plate, leaving the cake on the pan bottom. Mound the fool in the middle of the cake. Serve immediately.

Tasseography

READING TEA LEAVES

Tasseography is the ancient art of reading your fortunes in tea leaves. The finer the tea, the more detail you will find in the images.

Scatter half a teaspoon of fine loose tea into a white or light-coloured teacup.

Fill the cup with boiling water and let it steep for 3 minutes.

Drink your tea while you ponder ponderous thoughts.

Leave just enough water in the bottom of the cup to cover the loose tea.

Pick up your teacup and swirl it 3 times in the same direction and quickly dump the liquid into your saucer.

Wherever the leaves land is where you can begin to read them.

hare
The rough-and-tumble hare means you must follow your destiny to a travel destination.

diamond
Someone has a gift for you. You should probably invite them over for tea.

heart
There is love or friendship coming as long as you give your heart without losing your head.

teapot
A special guest is coming. You may want to put the kettle on.

book
An open book means you will discover the answer to a question. If it is closed you must investigate an answer to a question.

rabbit
Find some fleeting time to spend with family.

hat
Put your thinking hat on and find shelter from the maddening brainstorm.

crown
You will receive recognition for your achievements. Way to go!

mouse
Be cautious of things that are larger than you, but don't lose any sleep over it.

pig
Someone will eat more than their fair share of the tea biscuits. Have extras handy.

clock
You must not procrastinate. Fix something now and use the best butter possible.

Fizzy Iced Tea

Bubbles go straight from your mouth through your nose and into your head. They will lift your spirits and make you giddy with effervescently buoyantly bubbly fizzery.

Serves 4 bubbly buddies

Ingredients

- 1 Tbsp (15 mL) good-quality loose tea leaves or 3 to 4 tea bags—any kind
- ⅓ cup (85 mL) sugar or ¼ cup (60 mL) honey
- 4 cups (1 L) carbonated water, chilled
- thinly sliced lemon, for garnish (optional)

Put the tea leaves in a tea infuser and place in the teapot. Pour 2 cups (500 mL) of just-boiled water into the teapot; cover and let steep for 5 minutes. Remove the tea infuser and pour the tea into a pitcher that can be put into the refrigerator. Add the sugar and stir to dissolve. Refrigerate until well chilled.

Take the pitcher out of the refrigerator and slowly add the carbonated water. Serve immediately, over ice, with a thin slice of lemon, if you like.

Oat and Currant Scones

WITH LEMON CURD

Tea time is the perfect time for scones. Scone-time is the perfect
time for homemade curd. Curd-time is the perfect time for tea.
Lemon is a classic curd. Blackcurrant concentrate gives you a lovely
lavender-coloured curd. The lemon zest gives extra pow.

Makes about 1 dozen scones

Ingredients

SCONES

1½ cups (375 mL) all-purpose
    flour

½ cup (125 mL) quick or old-
    fashioned oats

2 Tbsp (30 mL) sugar

2 tsp (10 mL) baking powder

¼ tsp (1 mL) salt

⅓ cup cold butter, cut into
    chunks

1 large egg

½ cup (125 mL) half and half
    or 18% cream

½ cup (125 mL) currants or
    raisins

extra half and half or 18% cream,
    for brushing (optional)

coarse sugar, for sprinkling
    (optional)

LEMON CURD

6 large egg yolks

1 cup (250 mL) sugar

finely grated zest of a lemon

½ cup (125 mL) lemon juice or
    blackcurrant concentrate
    (such as Ribena)

½ cup (125 mL) butter, cut
    into pieces

Preheat the oven to 400°F (200°C) and line a baking sheet with
parchment paper.

TO MAKE THE SCONES In a medium bowl or the bowl of a food
processor, blend or pulse the flour, oats, sugar, baking powder
and salt until well blended. Add the butter and mix with a pastry
cutter or a fork, or pulse until the mixture is coarse, with lumps of
butter no bigger than a pea. If you used a food processor, dump the
mixture into a medium bowl.

In a small bowl, stir together the cream and egg with a fork.
Add, along with the currants, to the mixture; stir just until the
dough comes together.

On a lightly floured surface, pat the dough out to a ¾- to 1-inch
(2–2.5 cm) thickness; cut into rounds with a 2-inch (5 cm) cutter
or the rim of a glass and transfer to a greased or parchment-lined
baking sheet. Alternatively, pat the dough into a circle on the
sheet, then cut into wedges with a knife and pull them apart,
leaving at least 1 inch (2.5 cm) of space between them.

If you like, brush the tops of the scones with cream and sprinkle
with coarse sugar. Bake for 20 minutes, or until golden. Serve with
lemon curd, or jam and clotted cream.

TO MAKE THE LEMON CURD In a medium saucepan, whisk
together the egg yolks, sugar, lemon zest and juice. Set over
medium heat and cook, whisking almost constantly, until the
mixture comes to a boil and thickens.

Remove from the heat and stir in the butter. Set aside to cool.
Makes about 2 cups (500 mL).

Little Girl Bacon-and-Egg-Salad

Little girls eat eggs quite as much as serpents, you know.
However, serpents do not have fingers to pick up finger sandwiches,
so they prefer their eggs raw and whole.

Serves 6 to 8 little girls and no serpents

Ingredients

6-8 large eggs

¼-½ cup (60-125 mL) mayonnaise

1 tsp (5 mL) lemon juice

1 tsp (5 mL) Dijon or grainy mustard

salt and ground black pepper to taste

3-4 slices bacon, cooked until crisp and crumbled

1 green onion, finely chopped

2 Tbsp (30 mL) chopped fresh basil (optional)

6 slices white sandwich bread

soft butter

spring greens, leaf lettuce or pea shoots

Place the eggs in a medium saucepan, cover with cold water and bring to a boil. Cook, uncovered, for 10 minutes. Drain, then set the pan in the sink and run cold water over the eggs to stop them from cooking. Let them sit in the water until cool enough to handle.

Peel the eggs and roughly chop them—it's easy to do this in a bowl, using a whisk or pastry blender. Add the mayonnaise, lemon juice, mustard and salt and pepper to taste. Stir in the crumbled bacon, green onion and basil (if using).

Spread the sliced bread with butter, then with the egg salad, and top with the spring greens. Cut off the crusts, if you like, and cut each sandwich into quarters, squares or fingers to serve for tea.

No-Wine Jellies

It is not very civil to offer someone something that is not what it is supposedly supposed to be . . . at least one would suppose. Since there is no time for wine at a tea party, enjoy these juicy jellies that have no wine.

Makes about 60 jellies

Ingredients

1½ cups (375 mL) apple juice (or other fruit juice, except pineapple)

2 cups (500 mL) sugar

2 cups (500 mL) grape jelly

¼ cup (60 mL) powdered plain gelatin (or 4 packets)

extra sugar, for dusting

Alice's advice

Use any kind of fruit juice that makes your mouth water and turn it into a bouncy fruit juice jelly; just avoid pineapple, as it sometimes gets cranky and refuses to set. And don't use wine, because it isn't very civil to offer wine at a tea party, especially if there isn't any.

In a medium saucepan, combine 1 cup (250 mL) of the juice with the sugar and jelly. Bring to a simmer over medium heat, stirring until the sugar dissolves.

Meanwhile, in a small bowl or measuring cup, stir the gelatin into the remaining ½ cup (125 mL) of juice and let stand for a few minutes to soften; it will have the texture of applesauce. Whisk it into the hot jelly mixture, stirring until completely melted and smooth. Remove the pot from the heat and let it stand for a few minutes to cool slightly; skim off any foam that rises to the surface with a large spoon.

Pour the warm mixture into an 8-inch (20 cm) square baking pan that has been lined with plastic wrap and then sprayed with nonstick spray. Let sit at room temperature until cool, then cover and refrigerate for 2 hours or overnight, until firm.

Pour some sugar into a shallow dish. Cut the jelled mixture into 1-inch (2.5 cm) squares and toss in the sugar to coat.

CHAPTER 8

The Queen's Croquet-Ground

A large rose-tree stood near the entrance of the garden: the roses growing on it were white, but there were three gardeners at it, busily painting them red. Alice thought this a very curious thing, and she went nearer to watch them, and, just as she came up to them, she heard one of them say, "Look out now, Five! Don't go splashing paint over me like that!"

"I couldn't help it," said Five, in a sulky tone. "Seven jogged my elbow."

On which Seven looked up and said, "That's right, Five! Always lay the blame on others!"

"*You'd* better not talk!" said Five. "I heard the Queen say only yesterday you deserved to be beheaded!"

"What for?" said the one who had spoken first.

"That's none of *your* business, Two!" said Seven.

"Yes, it *is* his business!" said Five, "and I'll tell him—it was for bringing the cook tulip-roots instead of onions."

Seven flung down his brush, and had just begun, "Well, of all the unjust things—" when his eye chanced to fall upon Alice, as she stood watching them, and he checked himself suddenly: the others looked round also, and all of them bowed low.

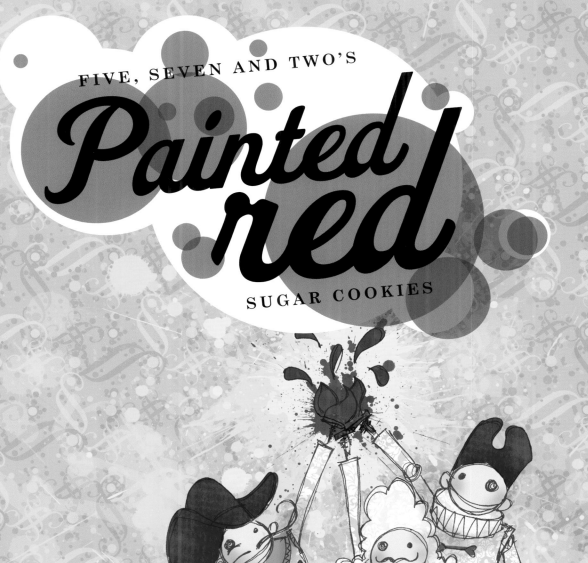

FIVE, SEVEN AND TWO'S

Painted red

SUGAR COOKIES

Painted-Red Sugar Cookies

If you make a mistake, don't lose your head. A little paint can
fix it up and if that fails, brush up on your cookie-baking.
It's more difficult to execute someone who has just given you cookies,
so stack the deck in your favour . . .

Makes 2 to 3 dozen cookies

Ingredients

COOKIES

⅓ cup (85 mL) butter, at room
    temperature

2 Tbsp (30 mL) canola or other
    mild vegetable oil

¾ cup (185 mL) sugar

grated zest of a lemon
    (optional)

1 large egg

2 tsp (10 mL) vanilla

1½ cups (375 mL) all-purpose
    flour

1 tsp (5 mL) baking powder

¼ tsp (1 mL) salt

PAINT

1 egg yolk

a few drops red food colouring

Alice's advice

Egg-yolk cookie "paint" cooks
dry and glossy—not sticky
like regular frosting—and you
have far more control with a
paintbrush than an icing bag.
Try making an entire palette
of colours in small ramekins,
adding a few drops of food
colouring per egg yolk.

TO MAKE THE COOKIES In a large bowl, beat the butter, oil,
sugar and lemon zest (if using) with an electric mixer until pale
and light; add the egg and vanilla and beat for a minute, until
smooth and well blended.

In a small bowl, stir together the flour, baking powder and salt.
Add to the sugar mixture and stir by hand or beat on low speed
just until you have a soft dough. Shape the dough into a disc, wrap
in plastic and refrigerate for half an hour.

When you're ready to bake, preheat the oven to 350°F (180°C).
On a lightly floured surface, roll the dough out to about ⅛-inch
(3 mm) thick. Cut the cookies into card shapes—or flowers, hearts,
spades or a combination of shapes—and place 1 inch (2.5 cm) apart
on a parchment-lined baking sheet.

TO MAKE THE PAINT Put the egg yolk in a small dish and add
a few drops of food colouring. Mix with a fork until well blended.
Use a small paintbrush to paint the unbaked cookies with the
red "paint."

Bake for 12 to 14 minutes, until the cookies are pale golden around
the edges and the paint is dry and glossy. Using a thin spatula,
transfer to a wire rack to cool.

"Would you tell me, please," said Alice, a little timidly, "why you are painting those roses?"

Five and Seven said nothing, but looked at Two. Two began, in a low voice, "Why, the fact is, you see, Miss, this here ought to have been a *red* rose-tree, and we put a white one in by mistake; and if the Queen was to find it out, we should all have our heads cut off, you know. So you see, Miss, we're doing our best, afore she comes, to—" At this moment Five, who had been anxiously looking across the garden, called out "The Queen! The Queen!" and the three gardeners instantly threw themselves flat upon their faces. There was a sound of many footsteps, and Alice looked round, eager to see the Queen.

First came ten soldiers carrying clubs; these were all shaped like the three gardeners, oblong and flat, with their hands and feet at the corners: next the ten courtiers; these were ornamented all over with diamonds, and walked two and two, as the soldiers did. After these came the royal children; there were ten of them, and the little dears came jumping merrily along, hand in hand, in couples: they were all ornamented with hearts. Next came the guests, mostly Kings and Queens, and among them Alice recognised the White Rabbit: it was talking in a hurried nervous manner, smiling at everything that was said, and went by without noticing her. Then followed the Knave of Hearts, carrying the King's crown on a crimson velvet cushion; and, last of all this grand procession, came THE KING AND QUEEN OF HEARTS.

Alice was rather doubtful whether she ought not to lie down on her face like the three gardeners, but she could not remember ever having heard of such a rule at processions; "and besides, what would be the use of a procession," thought she, "if people had all to lie down on their faces, so that they couldn't see it?" So she stood where she was, and waited.

When the procession came opposite to Alice, they all stopped and looked at her, and the Queen said, severely, "Who is this?" She said it to the Knave of Hearts, who only bowed and smiled in reply.

"Idiot!" said the Queen, tossing her head impatiently; and, turning to Alice, she went on, "What's your name, child?"

"My name is Alice, so please your Majesty," said Alice very politely; but she added, to herself, "Why, they're only a pack of cards, after all. I needn't be afraid of them!"

"And who are *these*?" said the Queen, pointing to the three gardeners who were lying round the rose-tree; for, you see, as they were lying on their faces, and the pattern on their backs was the same as the rest of the pack, she could not tell whether they were gardeners, or soldiers, or courtiers, or three of her own children.

"How should *I* know?" said Alice, surprised at her own courage. "It's no business of *mine*."

The Queen turned crimson with fury, and, after glaring at her for a moment like a wild beast, began screaming "Off with her head! Off with—"

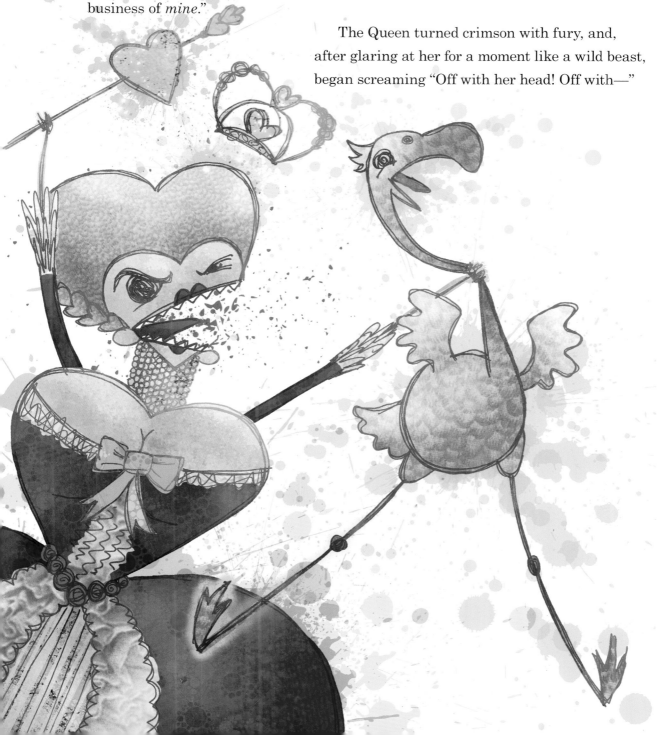

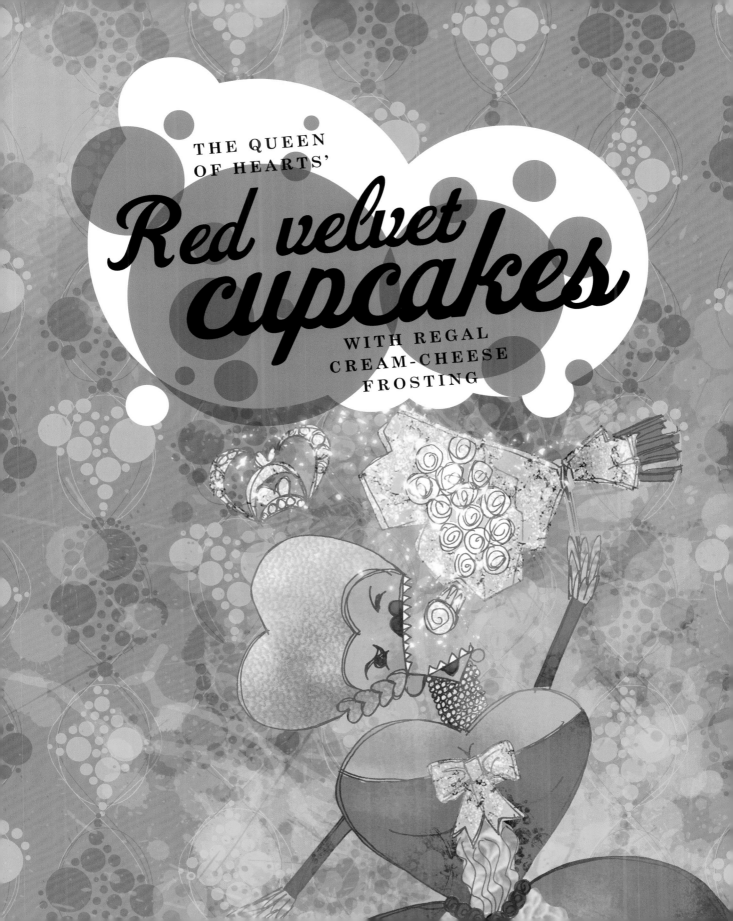

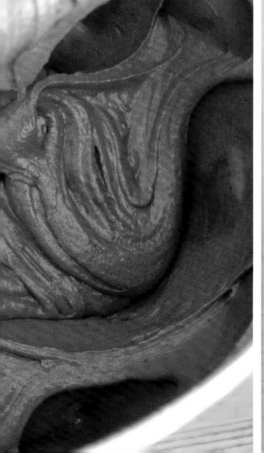

THE QUEEN OF HEARTS'
Red Velvet Cupcakes
WITH REGAL CREAM-CHEESE FROSTING

To win the Queen's heart, bake her a dozen red velvet cupcakes
and accessorize them with pristine regal frosting.

Makes 1 dozen cupcakes or 2 ½ dozen mini cupcakes

Ingredients

CUPCAKES

1½ cups (375 mL) flour

1 cup (250 mL) sugar

2-3 Tbsp (30-45 mL) cocoa powder

2 tsp (10 mL) baking powder

½ tsp (2 mL) baking soda

¼ tsp (1 mL) salt

¾ cup (185 mL) milk

1 tsp (5 mL) white vinegar

½ cup (125 mL) mild vegetable oil or melted butter

2 large eggs

2-3 tsp (10-15 mL) red food colouring

1 tsp (5 mL) vanilla

½ cup (125 mL) chocolate chips (optional)

REGAL CREAM-CHEESE FROSTING

¼ cup (60 mL) butter, softened

1 pkg (8 oz/250 g) cream cheese

2-3 cups (500-750 mL) icing sugar

2 Tbsp (30 mL) milk

1 tsp (5 mL) vanilla

TO MAKE THE CUPCAKES In a medium bowl, whisk together the flour, sugar, cocoa, baking powder, baking soda and salt.

In a large bowl, whisk together the milk and vinegar; set aside for 5 minutes. Whisk in the oil, eggs, red food colouring and vanilla. Add the dry ingredients and chocolate chips (if using) and stir just until well blended.

Fill paper-lined muffin cups (or mini muffin cups) and bake for 20 to 25 minutes, or until domed and springy to the touch. Let cool for a few minutes before transferring to a wire rack to cool completely before frosting.

TO MAKE THE REGAL CREAM-CHEESE FROSTING In a large bowl, beat the butter and cream cheese with an electric mixer until creamy. Gradually add the icing sugar, milk and vanilla, beating until the mixture is well blended and smooth; add a little more sugar or milk if necessary to achieve a spreadable frosting.

Once the cakes are completely cooled, spread with frosting or pipe it on top. To get a swirled effect fit for a queen, spoon the frosting into a Ziplock bag. Seal the bag and snip off a corner, then squeeze out the icing, in a pattern, onto the cooled cupcakes.

Alice's advice

In red velvet cakes, the chocolate is dialed down to allow the colour to shine through. If you want a more intense flavour with a mild blush, use more cocoa powder; if you're aiming for a redder velvet cupcake, keep the cocoa powder down to 2 Tbsp (30 mL) and turn up the red food colouring.

"Nonsense!" said Alice, very loudly and decidedly, and the Queen was silent.

The King laid his hand upon her arm, and timidly said, "Consider, my dear: she is only a child!"

The Queen turned angrily away from him, and said to the Knave, "Turn them over!"

The Knave did so, very carefully, with one foot.

"Get up!" said the Queen, in a shrill, loud voice, and the three gardeners instantly jumped up, and began bowing to the King, the Queen, the royal children, and everybody else.

"Leave off that!" screamed the Queen. "You make me giddy." And then, turning to the rose-tree, she went on, "What *have* you been doing here?"

"May it please your Majesty," said Two, in a very humble tone, going down on one knee as he spoke, "we were trying—"

"*I* see!" said the Queen, who had meanwhile been examining the roses. "Off with their heads!" and the procession moved on, three of the soldiers remaining behind to execute the unfortunate gardeners, who ran to Alice for protection.

"You shan't be beheaded!" said Alice, and she put them into a large flower-pot that stood near. The three soldiers wandered about for a minute or two, looking for them, and then quietly marched off after the others.

"Are their heads off?" shouted the Queen.

"Their heads are gone, if it please your Majesty!" the soldiers shouted in reply.

"That's right!" shouted the Queen. "Can you play croquet?"

The soldiers were silent, and looked at Alice, as the question was evidently meant for her.

"Yes!" shouted Alice.

"Come on, then!" roared the Queen, and Alice joined the procession, wondering very much what would happen next.

"It's—it's a very fine day!" said a timid voice at her side. She was walking by the White Rabbit, who was peeping anxiously into her face.

"Very," said Alice, "Where's the Duchess?"

"Hush! Hush!" said the Rabbit in a low, hurried tone. He looked anxiously over his shoulder as he spoke, and then raised himself upon tiptoe, put his mouth close to her ear, and whispered, "She's under sentence of execution."

"What for?" said Alice.

"Did you say 'What a pity!'?" the Rabbit asked.

"No, I didn't," said Alice; "I don't think it's at all a pity. I said 'What for?'"

"She boxed the Queen's ears—" the Rabbit began. Alice gave a little scream of laughter. "Oh, hush!" the Rabbit whispered in a frightened tone. "The Queen will hear you! You see, she came rather late, and the Queen said—"

"Get to your places!" shouted the Queen in a voice of thunder, and people began running about in all directions, tumbling up against each other; however, they got settled down in a minute or two, and the game began.

Alice thought she had never seen such a curious croquet-ground in her life: it was all ridges and furrows; the croquet balls were live hedgehogs, the mallets live flamingoes, and the soldiers had to double themselves up and stand on their hands and feet, to make the arches.

The chief difficulty Alice found at first was in managing her flamingo: she succeeded in getting its body tucked away, comfortably enough, under her arm, with its legs hanging down, but generally, just as she had got its neck nicely straightened out, and was going to give the hedgehog a blow with its head, it *would* twist itself round and look up in her face, with such a puzzled expression that she could not help bursting out laughing: and, when she had got its head down, and was going to begin again, it was very provoking to find that the hedgehog had unrolled itself, and was in the act of crawling away: besides all this, there was generally a ridge or furrow in the way wherever she wanted to send the hedgehog to, and, as the doubled-up soldiers were always getting up and walking off to other parts of the ground, Alice soon came to the conclusion that it was a very difficult game indeed.

The players all played at once, without waiting for turns, quarrelling all the while, and fighting for the hedgehogs; and in a very short time the Queen was in a furious passion, and went stamping about, and shouting "Off with his head!" or "Off with her head!" about once in a minute.

Alice began to feel very uneasy: to be sure, she had not as yet had any dispute with the Queen, but she knew that it might happen any minute, "and then," thought she, "what would become of me? They're dreadfully fond of beheading people here: the great wonder is, that there's any one left alive!"

She was looking about for some way of escape, and wondering whether she could get away without being seen, when she noticed a curious appearance in the air: it puzzled her very much at first, but after watching it a minute or two she made it out to be a grin, and she said to herself, "It's the Cheshire Cat: now I shall have somebody to talk to."

"How are you getting on?" said the Cat, as soon as there was mouth enough for it to speak with.

Alice waited till the eyes appeared, and then nodded. "It's no use speaking to it," she thought, "till its ears have come, or at least one of them." In another minute the whole head appeared, and then Alice put down her flamingo, and began an account of the game, feeling very glad she had someone to listen to her. The Cat seemed to think that there was enough of it now in sight, and no more of it appeared.

"I don't think they play at all fairly," Alice began, in rather a complaining tone, "and they all quarrel so dreadfully one can't hear oneself speak—and they

don't seem to have any rules in particular; at least, if there are, nobody attends to them—and you've no idea how confusing it is all the things being alive; for instance, there's the arch I've got to go through next walking about at the other end of the ground—and I should have croqueted the Queen's hedgehog just now, only it ran away when it saw mine coming!"

"How do you like the Queen?" said the Cat in a low voice.

"Not at all," said Alice: "she's so extremely—" Just then she noticed that the Queen was close behind her, listening: so she went on, "—likely to win, that it's hardly worth while finishing the game."

The Queen smiled and passed on.

"Who *are* you talking to?" said the King, coming up to Alice, and looking at the Cat's head with great curiosity.

"It's a friend of mine—a Cheshire Cat," said Alice: "allow me to introduce it."

"I don't like the look of it at all," said the King: "however, it may kiss my hand, if it likes."

"I'd rather not," the Cat remarked.

"Don't be impertinent," said the King, "and don't look at me like that!" He got behind Alice as he spoke.

"A cat may look at a king," said Alice. "I've read that in some book, but I don't remember where."

"Well, it must be removed," said the King very decidedly; and he called to the Queen, who was passing at the moment, "My dear! I wish you would have this cat removed!"

The Queen had only one way of settling all difficulties, great or small. "Off with his head!" she said, without even looking round.

"I'll fetch the executioner myself," said the King eagerly, and he hurried off.

Alice thought she might as well go back and see how the game was going on, as she heard the Queen's voice in the distance, screaming with passion. She had

already heard her sentence three of the players to be executed for having missed their turns, and she did not like the look of things at all, as the game was in such confusion that she never knew whether it was her turn or not. So she went in search of her hedgehog.

The hedgehog was engaged in a fight with another hedgehog, which seemed to Alice an excellent opportunity for croqueting one of them with the other: the only difficulty was, that her flamingo was gone across to the other side of the garden, where Alice could see it trying in a helpless sort of way to fly up into a tree.

By the time she had caught the flamingo and brought it back, the fight was over, and both the hedgehogs were out of sight: "but it doesn't matter much," thought Alice, "as all the arches are gone from this side of the ground." So she tucked it away under her arm, that it might not escape again, and went back for a little more conversation with her friend.

When she got back to the Cheshire Cat, she was surprised to find quite a large crowd collected round it: there was a dispute going on between the executioner, the King, and the Queen, who were all talking at once, while all the rest were quite silent, and looked very uncomfortable.

The moment Alice appeared, she was appealed to by all three to settle the question, and they repeated their arguments to her, though, as they all spoke at once, she found it very hard to make out exactly what they said.

The executioner's argument was, that you couldn't cut off a head unless there was a body to cut it off from: that he had never had to do such a thing before, and he wasn't going to begin at *his* time of life.

The King's argument was, that anything that had a head could be beheaded, and that you weren't to talk nonsense.

The Queen's argument was that, if something wasn't done about it in less than no time, she'd have everybody executed, all round. (It was this last remark that had made the whole party look so grave and anxious.)

Alice could think of nothing else to say but "It belongs to the Duchess: you'd better ask *her* about it."

"She's in prison," the Queen said to the executioner: "fetch her here." And the executioner went off like an arrow.

The Cat's head began fading away the moment he was gone, and, by the time he had come back with the Duchess, it had entirely disappeared; so the King and the executioner ran wildly up and down looking for it, while the rest of the party went back to the game.

CHAPTER 9

The Mock Turtle's Story

"Y ou can't think how glad I am to see you again, you dear old thing!" said the Duchess, as she tucked her arm affectionately into Alice's, and they walked off together.

Alice was very glad to find her in such a pleasant temper, and thought to herself that perhaps it was only the pepper that had made her so savage when they met in the kitchen.

"When *I'm* a Duchess," she said to herself (not in a very hopeful tone though), "I won't have any pepper in my kitchen *at all*. Soup does very well without—Maybe it's always pepper that makes people hot-tempered," she went on, very much pleased at having found out a new kind of rule, "and vinegar that makes them sour—and camomile that makes them bitter—and—and barley-sugar and such things that make children sweet-tempered. I only wish people knew *that*: then they wouldn't be so stingy about it, you know—"

She had quite forgotten the Duchess by this time, and was a little startled when she heard her voice close to her ear. "You're thinking about something, my dear, and that makes you forget to talk. I can't tell you just now what the moral of that is, but I shall remember it in a bit."

"Perhaps it hasn't one," Alice ventured to remark.

"Tut, tut, child!" said the Duchess. "Everything's got a moral, if only you can find it." And she squeezed herself up closer to Alice's side as she spoke.

Alice did not much like keeping so close to her: first, because the Duchess was *very* ugly; and secondly, because she was exactly the right height to rest her chin upon Alice's shoulder, and it was an uncomfortably sharp chin. However, she did not like to be rude: so she bore it as well as she could.

"The game's going on rather better now," she said, by way of keeping up the conversation a little.

"'Tis so," said the Duchess: "and the moral of that is—'Oh, 'tis love, 'tis love, that makes the world go round!'"

"Somebody said," Alice whispered, "that it's done by everybody minding their own business!"

"Ah, well! It means much the same thing," said the Duchess, digging her sharp little chin into Alice's shoulder as she added, "and the moral of *that* is—'Take care of the sense, and the sounds will take care of themselves.'"

"How fond she is of finding morals in things!" Alice thought to herself.

"I dare say you're wondering why I don't put my arm round your waist," the Duchess said, after a pause: "the reason is, that I'm doubtful about the temper of your flamingo. Shall I try the experiment?"

"He might bite," Alice cautiously replied, not feeling at all anxious to have the experiment tried.

"Very true," said the Duchess: "flamingoes and mustard both bite. And the moral of that is—'Birds of a feather flock together.'"

"Only mustard isn't a bird," Alice remarked.

"Right, as usual," said the Duchess: "what a clear way you have of putting things!"

"It's a mineral, I *think*," said Alice.

"Of course it is," said the Duchess, who seemed ready to agree to everything that Alice said; "there's a large mustard-mine near here. And the moral of that is—'The more there is of mine, the less there is of yours.'"

"Oh, I know!" exclaimed Alice, who had not attended to this last remark, "it's a vegetable. It doesn't look like one, but it is."

"I quite agree with you," said the Duchess; "and the moral of that is—'Be what you would seem to be'—or if you'd like it put more simply—'Never imagine yourself not to be otherwise than what it might appear to others that what you were or might have been was not otherwise than what you had been would have appeared to them to be otherwise.'"

"I think I should understand that better," Alice said very politely, "if I had it written down: but I can't quite follow it as you say it."

"That's nothing to what I could say if I chose," the Duchess replied, in a pleased tone.

"Pray don't trouble yourself to say it any longer than that," said Alice.

"Oh, don't talk about trouble!" said the Duchess. "I make you a present of everything I've said as yet."

"A cheap sort of present!" thought Alice. "I'm glad people don't give birthday presents like that!" But she did not venture to say it out loud.

"Thinking again?" the Duchess asked, with another dig of her sharp little chin.

"I've a right to think," said Alice sharply, for she was beginning to feel a little worried.

"Just about as much right," said the Duchess, "as pigs have to fly; and the m—"

But here, to Alice's great surprise, the Duchess's voice died away, even in the middle of her favourite word 'moral,' and the arm that was linked into hers began to tremble. Alice looked up, and there stood the Queen in front of them, with her arms folded, frowning like a thunderstorm.

"A fine day, your Majesty!" the Duchess began in a low, weak voice.

"Now, I give you fair warning," shouted the Queen, stamping on the ground as she spoke; "either you or your head must be off, and that in about half no time! Take your choice!"

The Duchess took her choice, and was gone in a moment.

"Let's go on with the game," the Queen said to Alice; and Alice was too much frightened to say a word, but slowly followed her back to the croquet-ground.

The other guests had taken advantage of the Queen's absence, and were resting in the shade: however, the moment they saw her, they hurried back to the game, the Queen merely remarking that a moment's delay would cost them their lives.

All the time they were playing the Queen never left off quarrelling with the

other players, and shouting "Off with his head!" or "Off with her head!" Those whom she sentenced were taken into custody by the soldiers, who of course had to leave off being arches to do this, so that, by the end of half an hour or so there were no arches left, and all the players, except the King, the Queen, and Alice, were in custody, and under sentence of execution.

Then the Queen left off, quite out of breath, and said to Alice, "Have you seen the Mock Turtle yet?"

"No," said Alice. "I don't even know what a Mock Turtle is."

"It's the thing Mock Turtle Soup is made from," said the Queen.

"I never saw one, or heard of one," said Alice.

"Come on, then," said the Queen, "and he shall tell you his history,"

As they walked off together, Alice heard the King say in a low voice, to the company generally, "You are all pardoned." "Come, *that's* a good thing!" she said to herself, for she had felt quite unhappy at the number of executions the Queen had ordered.

They very soon came upon a Gryphon, lying fast asleep in the sun. (If you don't know what a Gryphon is, look at the picture.) "Up, lazy thing!" said the Queen, "and take this young lady to see the Mock Turtle, and to hear his history. I must go back and see after some executions I have ordered;" and she walked off, leaving Alice alone with the Gryphon. Alice did not quite like the look of the creature, but on the whole she thought it would be quite as safe to stay with it as to go after that savage Queen: so she waited.

The Gryphon sat up and rubbed its eyes: then it watched the Queen till she was out of sight: then it chuckled. "What fun!" said the Gryphon, half to itself, half to Alice.

"What is the fun?" said Alice.

"Why, *she*," said the Gryphon. "It's all her fancy, that: they never executes nobody, you know. Come on!"

"Everybody says 'come on!' here," thought Alice, as she went slowly after it: "I never was so ordered about before, in all my life, never!"

They had not gone far before they saw the Mock Turtle in the distance, sitting sad and lonely on a little ledge of rock, and, as they came nearer, Alice could hear him sighing as if his heart would break. She pitied him deeply. "What is his sorrow?" she asked the Gryphon. And the Gryphon answered, very nearly in the same words as before, "It's all his fancy, that: he hasn't got no sorrow, you know. Come on!"

So they went up to the Mock Turtle, who looked at them with large eyes full of tears, but said nothing.

"This here young lady," said the Gryphon, "she wants for to know your history, she do."

"I'll tell it her," said the Mock Turtle in a deep, hollow tone. "Sit down, both of you, and don't speak a word till I've finished."

So they sat down, and nobody spoke for some minutes. Alice thought to herself, "I don't see how he can ever finish, if he doesn't begin." But she waited patiently.

"Once," said the Mock Turtle at last, with a deep sigh, "I was a real Turtle."

These words were followed by a very long silence, broken only by an occasional exclamation of "Hjckrrh!" from the Gryphon, and the constant heavy sobbing of the Mock Turtle. Alice was very nearly getting up and saying, "Thank you, sir, for your

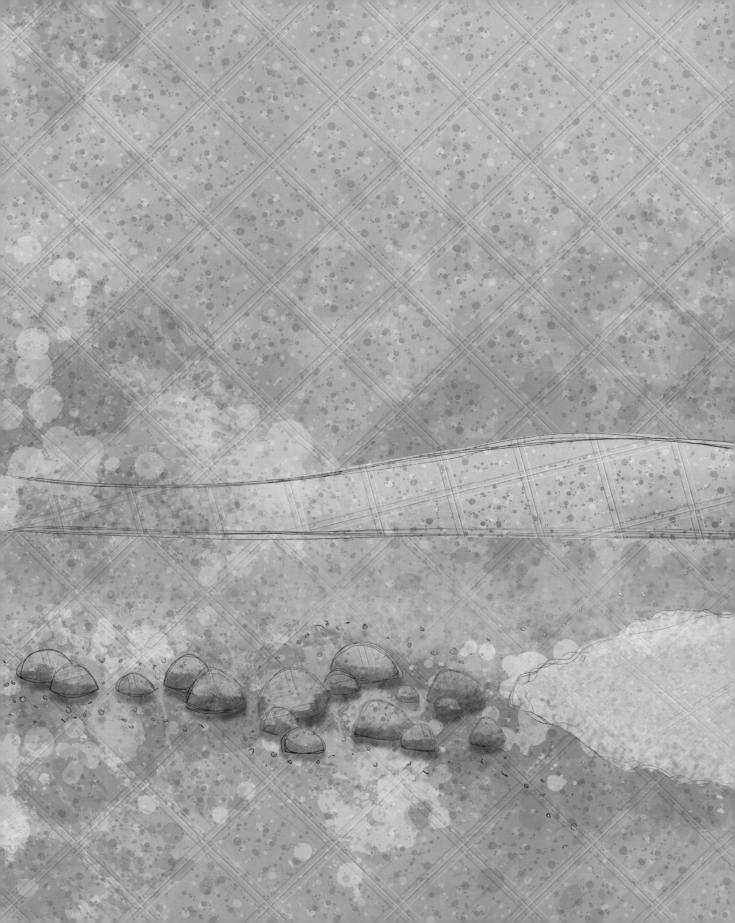

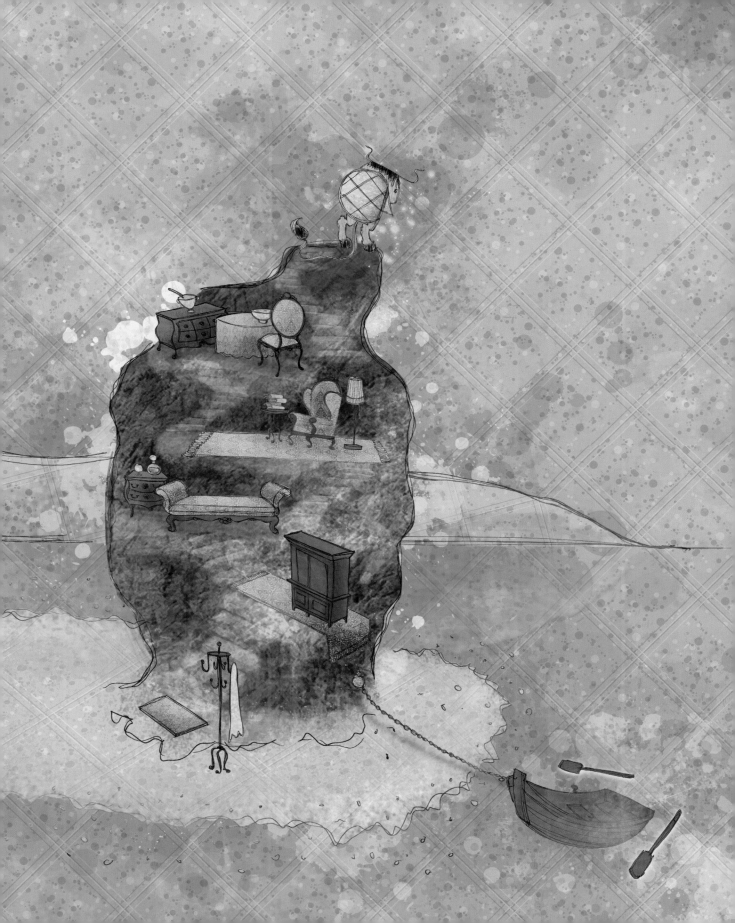

Mock Turtle Chocolates

Stop a mocked turtle's slobbery sobbery with sweetness.
No turtle is an island, and even a lonely turtle will be happy with the
friendly gesture of chewy chocolate treats. It will make you sigh deeply
and weep tears of joy when you try these sweet mock turtles.

Makes about 2 dozen tasty turtles

Ingredients

- 1½ cups (250 mL) pecan halves
- 24 individually wrapped square caramels
- 1 bar (3 oz/90 g) dark chocolate, broken into about 24 pieces

Preheat the oven to 350°F (180°C).

On a parchment-lined baking sheet, arrange the pecan halves in groups of four, all pointing away from each other, like the legs of a turtle. Unwrap the caramels and place one on top of each cluster, right in the middle.

Bake for 8 to 10 minutes, or until the caramel softens and starts to melt. Remove from the oven and place a square of chocolate on top of each caramel, pressing lightly so that the caramel oozes out a bit on the sides. If the turtles have spread out too much, you can push the pecans back together while the caramel is still soft.

Let stand at room temperature for 10 to 20 minutes, or until cooled and set.

interesting story," but she could not help thinking there *must* be more to come, so she sat still and said nothing.

"When we were little," the Mock Turtle went on at last, more calmly, though still sobbing a little now and then, "we went to school in the sea. The master was an old Turtle—we used to call him Tortoise—"

"Why did you call him Tortoise, if he wasn't one?" Alice asked.

"We called him Tortoise because he taught us," said the Mock Turtle angrily, "really you are very dull!"

"You ought to be ashamed of yourself for asking such a simple question," added the Gryphon; and then they both sat silent and looked at poor Alice, who felt ready to sink into the earth. At last the Gryphon said to the Mock Turtle, "Drive on, old fellow! Don't be all day about it!" and he went on in these words—

"Yes, we went to school in the sea, though you mayn't believe it—"

"I never said I didn't!" interrupted Alice.

"You did," said the Mock Turtle.

"Hold your tongue!" added the Gryphon, before Alice could speak again. The Mock Turtle went on.

"We had the best of educations—in fact, we went to school every day—"

"*I've* been to a day-school, too," said Alice; "you needn't be so proud as all that."

"With extras?" asked the Mock Turtle, a little anxiously.

"Yes," said Alice: "we learned French and music."

"And washing?" said the Mock Turtle.

"Certainly not!" said Alice indignantly.

"Ah! Then yours wasn't a really good school," said the Mock Turtle in a tone of great relief. "Now at *ours* they had at the end of the bill, 'French, music, *and washing*—extra.'"

"You couldn't have wanted it much," said Alice; "living at the bottom of the sea."

"I couldn't afford to learn it," said the Mock Turtle with a sigh. "I only took the regular course."

"What was that?" inquired Alice.

"Reeling and Writhing, of course, to begin with," the Mock Turtle replied; "and then the different branches of Arithmetic—Ambition, Distraction, Uglification, and Derision."

"I never heard of 'Uglification,'" Alice ventured to say. "What is it?"

The Gryphon lifted up both its paws in surprise. "Never heard of uglifying!" it exclaimed. "You know what to beautify is, I suppose?"

"Yes," said Alice doubtfully: "it means—to—make—anything—prettier."

"Well, then," the Gryphon went on, "if you don't know what to uglify is, you *are* a simpleton."

Alice did not feel encouraged to ask any more questions about it: so she turned to the Mock Turtle, and said "What else had you to learn?"

"Well, there was Mystery," the Mock Turtle replied, counting off the subjects on his flappers, "—Mystery, ancient and modern, with Seaography: then Drawling—the Drawling-master was an old conger-eel, that used to come once a week: *he* taught us Drawling, Stretching, and Fainting in Coils."

"What was *that* like?" said Alice.

"Well, I can't show it you, myself," the Mock Turtle said: "I'm too stiff. And the Gryphon never learnt it."

"Hadn't time," said the Gryphon: "I went to the Classical master, though. He was an old crab, *he* was."

"I never went to him," the Mock Turtle said with a sigh. "he taught Laughing and Grief, they used to say."

"So he did, so he did," said the Gryphon, sighing in his turn; and both creatures hid their faces in their paws.

"And how many hours a day did you do lessons?" said Alice, in a hurry to change the subject.

"Ten hours the first day," said the Mock Turtle: "nine the next, and so on."

"What a curious plan!" exclaimed Alice.

"That's the reason they're called lessons," the Gryphon remarked: "because they lessen from day to day."

This was quite a new idea to Alice, and she thought it over a little before she made her next remark. "Then the eleventh day must have been a holiday?"

"Of course it was," said the Mock Turtle.

"And how did you manage on the twelfth?" Alice went on eagerly.

"That's enough about lessons," the Gryphon interrupted in a very decided tone. "Tell her something about the games now."

CHAPTER 10

The Lobster Quadrille

The Mock Turtle sighed deeply, and drew the back of one flapper across his eyes. He looked at Alice and tried to speak, but, for a minute or two, sobs choked his voice. "Same as if he had a bone in his throat," said the Gryphon; and it set to work shaking him and punching him in the back. At last the Mock Turtle recovered his voice, and, with tears running down his cheeks, he went on again:—

"You may not have lived much under the sea—" ("I haven't," said Alice)— "and perhaps you were never even introduced to a lobster—" (Alice began to say "I once tasted—" but checked herself hastily, and said "No, never") "—so you can have no idea what a delightful thing a Lobster-Quadrille is!"

"No, indeed," said Alice. "What sort of a dance is it?"

"Why," said the Gryphon, "you first form into a line along the seashore—"

"Two lines!" cried the Mock Turtle. "Seals, turtles, salmon, and so on; then, when you've cleared all the jelly-fish out of the way—"

"*That* generally takes some time," interrupted the Gryphon.

"—you advance twice—"

"Each with a lobster as a partner!" cried the Gryphon.

"Of course," the Mock Turtle said: "advance twice, set to partners—"

"—change lobsters, and retire in same order," continued the Gryphon.

"Then, you know," the Mock Turtle went on, "you throw the—"

"The lobsters!" shouted the Gryphon, with a bound into the air.

"—as far out to sea as you can—"

"Swim after them!" screamed the Gryphon.

"Turn a somersault in the sea!" cried the Mock Turtle, capering wildly about.

"Change lobsters again!" yelled the Gryphon at the top of its voice.

"Back to land again, and—that's all the first figure," said the Mock Turtle, suddenly dropping his voice; and the two creatures, who had been jumping about like mad things all this time, sat down again very sadly and quietly, and looked at Alice.

"It must be a very pretty dance," said Alice timidly.

"Would you like to see a little of it?" said the Mock Turtle.

"Very much indeed," said Alice.

"Come, let's try the first figure!" said the Mock Turtle to the Gryphon. "We can do without lobsters, you know. Which shall sing?"

"Oh, *you* sing," said the Gryphon. "I've forgotten the words."

So they began solemnly dancing round and round Alice, every now and then treading on her toes when they passed too close, and waving their forepaws to mark the time, while the Mock Turtle sang this, very slowly and sadly:—

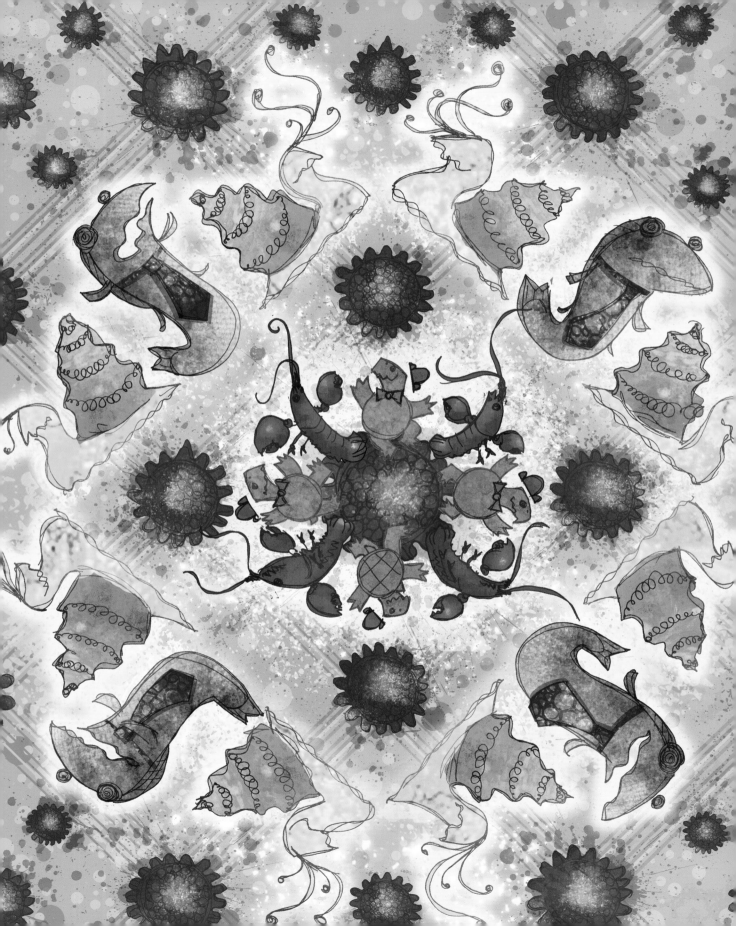

"Will you walk a little faster?" said a whiting to a snail,
"There's a porpoise close behind us, and he's treading on my tail.
See how eagerly the lobsters and the turtles all advance!
They are waiting on the shingle—will you come and join the dance?
  Will you, won't you, will you, won't you, will you join the dance?
  Will you, won't you, will you, won't you, won't you join the dance?

"You can really have no notion how delightful it will be
When they take us up and throw us, with the lobsters, out to sea!"
But the snail replied "Too far, too far!" and gave a look askance—
Said he thanked the whiting kindly, but he would not join the dance.
  Would not, could not, would not, could not, would not join the dance.
  Would not, could not, would not, could not, could not join the dance.

"What matters it how far we go?" his scaly friend replied.
"There is another shore, you know, upon the other side.
The further off from England the nearer is to France—
Then turn not pale, beloved snail, but come and join the dance.
  Will you, won't you, will you, won't you, will you join the dance?
  Will you, won't you, will you, won't you, won't you join the dance?"

"Thank you, it's a very interesting dance to watch," said Alice, feeling very glad that it was over at last: "and I do so like that curious song about the whiting!"

"Oh, as to the whiting," said the Mock Turtle, "they—you've seen them, of course?"

"Yes," said Alice, "I've often seen them at dinn—" she checked herself hastily.

"I don't know where Dinn may be," said the Mock Turtle; "but if you've seen them so often, of course you know what they're like."

"I believe so," Alice replied thoughtfully. "They have their tails in their mouths—and they're all over crumbs."

"You're wrong about the crumbs," said the Mock Turtle: "crumbs would all wash off in the sea. But they *have* their tails in their mouths; and the reason is—" here the Mock Turtle yawned and shut his eyes. "Tell her about the reason and all that," he said to the Gryphon.

Mini Lobster Rolls

Will you, won't you, will you, won't you, will you take the chance
To try a little lobster roll before you join the dance?
You can really have no notion how delightful it will be
When you make a little roll with the lobsters from the sea!

Serves 4 to 6

Ingredients

½ lb (250 g) cooked lobster, crab or shrimp meat, or a combination

¼ cup (60 mL) mayonnaise, or to taste

1 small celery stalk, finely chopped (with leaves)

2 Tbsp (30 mL) finely chopped parsley

1 green onion or a few chives, finely chopped

2 tsp (10 mL) lemon juice

salt and ground black pepper

4–6 small, soft white dinner rolls, uncut if possible

Crumble or chop the lobster into a medium bowl, picking out any bits of cartilage you come across. Add the mayonnaise, celery, parsley, green onion and lemon juice and gently stir to combine. Season with salt and pepper.

Cut a vertical slit in your rolls through the middle of the top, running lengthwise, leaving the bottom crust intact, and open them up. Stuff each roll with lobster mixture. If you like, cut each roll in half on a slight diagonal for smaller tea party pieces.

"The reason is," said the Gryphon, "that they *would* go with the lobsters to the dance. So they got thrown out to sea. So they had to fall a long way. So they got their tails fast in their mouths. So they couldn't get them out again. That's all."

"Thank you," said Alice, "it's very interesting. I never knew so much about a whiting before."

"I can tell you more than that, if you like," said the Gryphon. "Do you know why it's called a whiting?"

"I never thought about it," said Alice. "Why?"

"*It does the boots and shoes*," the Gryphon replied very solemnly.

Alice was thoroughly puzzled. "Does the boots and shoes!" she repeated in a wondering tone.

"Why, what are *your* shoes done with?" said the Gryphon. "I mean, what makes them so shiny?"

Alice looked down at them, and considered a little before she gave her answer. "They're done with blacking, I believe."

"Boots and shoes under the sea," the Gryphon went on in a deep voice, "are done with whiting. Now you know."

"And what are they made of?" Alice asked in a tone of great curiosity.

"Soles and eels, of course," the Gryphon replied, rather impatiently: "any shrimp could have told you that."

"If I'd been the whiting," said Alice, whose thoughts were still running on the song, "I'd have said to the porpoise, 'Keep back, please. We don't want *you* with us!'"

"They were obliged to have him with them," the Mock Turtle said. "No wise fish would go anywhere without a porpoise."

"Wouldn't it really?" said Alice in a tone of great surprise.

"Of course not," said the Mock Turtle. "Why, if a fish came to *me*, and told me he was going a journey, I should say 'With what porpoise?'"

"Don't you mean 'purpose'?" said Alice.

"I mean what I say," the Mock Turtle replied in an offended tone. And the Gryphon added "Come, let's hear some of *your* adventures."

"I could tell you my adventures—beginning from this morning," said Alice a little timidly: "but it's no use going back to yesterday, because I was a different person then."

"Explain all that," said the Mock Turtle.

"No, no! The adventures first," said the Gryphon in an impatient tone: "explanations take such a dreadful time."

So Alice began telling them her adventures from the time when she first saw the White Rabbit. She was a little nervous about it, just at first, the two creatures got so close to her, one on each side, and opened their eyes and mouths so *very* wide; but she gained courage as she went on. Her listeners were perfectly quiet till she got to the part about her repeating "*You are old, Father William*," to the Caterpillar, and the words all coming different, and then the Mock Turtle drew a long breath, and said, "That's very curious."

"It's all about as curious as it can be," said the Gryphon.

"It all came different!" the Mock Turtle repeated thoughtfully. "I should like to hear her try and repeat something now. Tell her to begin." He looked at the Gryphon as if he thought it had some kind of authority over Alice.

"Stand up and repeat '*Tis the voice of the sluggard*,'" said the Gryphon.

"How the creatures order one about, and make one repeat lessons!" thought Alice. "I might as well be at school at once." However, she got up, and began to repeat it, but her head was so full of the Lobster-Quadrille, that she hardly knew what she was saying; and the words came very queer indeed:—

"'Tis the voice of the Lobster: I heard him declare
'You have baked me too brown, I must sugar my hair.'
As a duck with its eyelids, so he with his nose
Trims his belt and his buttons, and turns out his toes.
When the sands are all dry, he is gay as a lark,
And will talk in contemptuous tones of the Shark:
But, when the tide rises and sharks are around,
His voice has a timid and tremulous sound."

"That's different from what *I* used to say when I was a child," said the Gryphon.

"Well, *I* never heard it before," said the Mock Turtle; "but it sounds uncommon nonsense."

Alice said nothing; she had sat down with her face in her hands, wondering if anything would *ever* happen in a natural way again.

"I should like to have it explained," said the Mock Turtle.

"She can't explain it," said the Gryphon hastily. "Go on with the next verse."

"But about his toes?" the Mock Turtle persisted. "How *could* he turn them out with his nose, you know?"

"It's the first position in dancing," Alice said; but she was dreadfully puzzled by the whole thing, and longed to change the subject.

"Go on with the next verse," the Gryphon repeated impatiently: "it begins '*I passed by his garden.*'"

Alice did not dare to disobey, though she felt sure it would all come wrong, and she went on in a trembling voice:—

> "I passed by his garden, and marked, with one eye,
> How the Owl and the Panther were sharing a pie:
> The Panther took pie-crust, and gravy, and meat,
> While the Owl had the dish as its share of the treat.
> When the pie was all finished, the Owl, as a boon,
> Was kindly permitted to pocket the spoon:
> While the Panther received knife and fork with a growl,
> And concluded the banquet by—"

"What *is* the use of repeating all that stuff," the Mock Turtle interrupted, "if you don't explain it as you go on? It's by far the most confusing thing *I* ever heard!"

"Yes, I think you'd better leave off," said the Gryphon, and Alice was only too glad to do so.

"Shall we try another figure of the Lobster-Quadrille?" the Gryphon went on. "Or would you like the Mock Turtle to sing you another song?"

"Oh, a song, please, if the Mock Turtle would be so kind," Alice replied, so eagerly that the Gryphon said, in a rather offended tone, "Hm! No accounting for tastes! Sing her '*Turtle Soup*,' will you, old fellow?"

The Mock Turtle sighed deeply, and began, in a voice choked with sobs, to sing this:—

"Beautiful Soup, so rich and green,
Waiting in a hot tureen!
Who for such dainties would not stoop?
Soup of the evening, beautiful Soup!
Soup of the evening, beautiful Soup!

Beau—ootiful Soo—oop!
Beau—ootiful Soo—oop!
Soo—oop of the e—e—evening,
Beautiful, beautiful Soup!

"Beautiful Soup! Who cares for fish,
Game, or any other dish?
Who would not give all else for two
pennyworth only of beautiful Soup?
Pennyworth only of beautiful Soup?

Beau—ootiful Soo—oop!
Beau—ootiful Soo—oop!
Soo—oop of the e—e—evening,
Beautiful, beauti—FUL SOUP!"

"Chorus again!" cried the Gryphon, and the Mock Turtle had just begun to repeat it, when a cry of "The trial's beginning!" was heard in the distance.

"Come on!" cried the Gryphon, and, taking Alice by the hand, it hurried off, without waiting for the end of the song.

"What trial is it?" Alice panted as she ran; but the Gryphon only answered "Come on!" and ran the faster, while more and more faintly came, carried on the breeze that followed them, the melancholy words:—

"Soo—oop of the e—e—evening,
Beautiful, beautiful Soup!"

Mock Turtle Soup

Turtle soup is made from a turtle. Mock turtle is made from a beef head.
This mockery of a mock turtle soup is made of neither
but it is rich and so green, waiting in a hot tureen.

Makes 4 to 6 bowls full

Ingredients

- 6 cups (1.5 L) chicken stock
- ½ cup (125 mL) small or medium pasta shells
- ½ lb (250 g) fresh Italian sausages (about 2)
- 2 large eggs
- ¼ cup (60 mL) grated Parmesan cheese, plus extra for serving
- 2 packed cups (500 mL) fresh spinach, roughly chopped

Bring the stock to a simmer in a medium pot set over medium-high heat. In another saucepan, cook the pasta shells according to package directions, until tender but still firm to the bite. (Alternatively, add an extra cup of water to the stock and boil the pasta in it—the broth will be cloudier due to the pasta starch.)

Squeeze the sausages out of their casings by twisting at ½-inch (1 cm) intervals, creating little balls of meat, and squeezing them into the simmering stock. Let cook for 3 to 4 minutes, until firm.

Meanwhile, whisk together the eggs and Parmesan cheese in a small bowl; drizzle into the simmering soup, stirring gently so that it doesn't completely blend in, but cooks in strands. Add the spinach and cook for another minute or two, until it wilts.

Season with salt and pepper, and serve with extra Parmesan cheese grated on top.

CHAPTER 11

Who Stole the Tarts?

he King and Queen of Hearts were seated on their throne when they arrived, with a great crowd assembled about them—all sorts of little birds and beasts, as well as the whole pack of cards: the Knave was standing before them, in chains, with a soldier on each side to guard him; and near the King was the White Rabbit, with a trumpet in one hand, and a scroll of parchment in the other. In the very middle of the court was a table, with a large dish of tarts upon it: they looked so good, that it made Alice quite hungry to look at them—"I wish they'd get the trial done," she thought, "and hand round the refreshments!" But there seemed to be no chance of this, so she began looking at everything about her, to pass away the time.

Alice had never been in a court of justice before, but she had read about them in books, and she was quite pleased to find that she knew the name of nearly everything there. "That's the judge," she said to herself, "because of his great wig."

The judge, by the way, was the King; and, as he wore his crown over the wig, he did not look at all comfortable, and it was certainly not becoming.

"And that's the jury-box," thought Alice; "and those twelve creatures" (she was obliged to say "creatures," you see, because some of them were animals, and some were birds), "I suppose they are the jurors." She said this last word two or three times over to herself, being rather proud of it: for she thought, and rightly too, that very few little girls of her age knew the meaning of it at all. However, "jurymen" would have done just as well.

The twelve jurors were all writing very busily on slates. "What are they doing?" Alice whispered to the Gryphon. "They can't have anything to put down yet, before the trial's begun."

"They're putting down their names," the Gryphon whispered in reply, "for fear they should forget them before the end of the trial."

"Stupid things!" Alice began in a loud, indignant voice; but she stopped herself hastily, for the White Rabbit cried out, "Silence in the court!" and the King put on his spectacles and looked anxiously round, to make out who was talking.

Alice could see, as well as if she were looking over their shoulders, that all the jurors were writing down "Stupid things!" on their slates, and she could even make out that one of them didn't know how to spell "stupid," and that he had to ask his neighbour to tell him. "A nice muddle their slates'll be in, before the trial's over!" thought Alice.

One of the jurors had a pencil that squeaked. This, of course, Alice could *not* stand, and she went round the court and got behind him, and very soon found an opportunity of taking it away. She did it so quickly that the poor little juror (it was Bill, the Lizard) could not make out at all what had become of it; so, after hunting all about for it, he was obliged to write with one finger for the rest of the day; and this was of very little use, as it left no mark on the slate.

"Herald, read the accusation!" said the King.

On this the White Rabbit blew three blasts on the trumpet, and then unrolled the parchment-scroll, and read as follows:—

> "The Queen of Hearts, she made some tarts,
>   All on a summer day:
> The Knave of Hearts, he stole those tarts
>   And took them quite away!"

THE QUEEN OF HEARTS' Jam TARTS

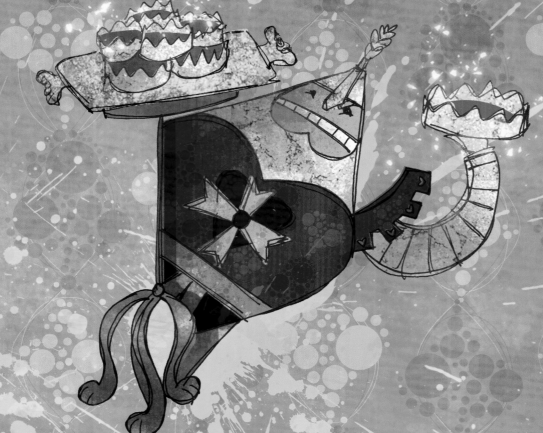

Jam Tarts

The evidence is overwhelming. The Queen of Hearts, she made some tarts, all on a summer day. The Knave of Hearts, he stole those tarts, and took them quite away! Who in this court can blame him?

Makes 2 to 3 dozen jam tarts

Ingredients

- 2¼ cups (560 mL) all-purpose flour
- 2 Tbsp (30 mL) sugar
- 1 tsp (2 mL) salt
- ½ cup (125 mL) butter, chilled and cubed
- ½ cup (125 mL) lard, chilled and cubed (or more butter)
- 1 tsp (5 mL) finely grated lemon zest (optional)
- 1 large egg
- 1 cup (250 mL) raspberry jam or other sweet preserve, such as marmalade
- 2 cups (500 mL) fresh raspberries (optional)

In a large bowl or in the bowl of a food processor, combine the flour, sugar and salt. Add the butter and lard and the lemon zest (if using). Blend with a pastry cutter or pulse in the food processor until the mixture has a mealy consistency, with some pieces of fat the size of small peas.

If you used a food processor, dump the flour mixture into a bowl. In a glass measuring cup, stir the egg with a fork, then add very cold water to make ½ cup (125 mL). Add to the flour mixture and stir just until the dough comes together. Divide the dough into two pieces and shape each into a disc; wrap in plastic wrap and refrigerate or freeze until needed.

When you're ready to assemble the tarts, preheat the oven to 350°F (180°C). On a lightly floured surface, roll one piece of dough out about ⅛-inch (3 mm) thick. Cut into rounds with a 2½- to 3-inch (6–8 cm) cookie cutter or the rim of a glass, and press into the bottom of ungreased muffin tins. Re-roll the scraps only once to get as many rounds as you can. Put a small spoonful of jam— a teaspoon or two—into each pastry cup.

Bake for 15 minutes, or until the pastry is pale golden and the jam is bubbly around the edges. Cool the tarts for 5 minutes in their tins before removing (you may need the help of a thin knife) to a wire rack to cool. Place a fresh raspberry upright on each tart, if you like.

"Consider your verdict," the King said to the jury.

"Not yet, not yet!" the Rabbit hastily interrupted. "There's a great deal to come before that!"

"Call the first witness," said the King; and the White Rabbit blew three blasts on the trumpet, and called out "First witness!"

The first witness was the Hatter. He came in with a teacup in one hand and a piece of bread-and-butter in the other. "I beg pardon, your Majesty," he began, "for bringing these in, but I hadn't quite finished my tea when I was sent for."

"You ought to have finished," said the King. "When did you begin?"

The Hatter looked at the March Hare, who had followed him into the court, arm-in-arm with the Dormouse. "Fourteenth of March, I *think* it was," he said.

"Fifteenth," said the March Hare.

"Sixteenth," said the Dormouse.

"Write that down," the King said to the jury; and the jury eagerly wrote down all three dates on their slates, and then added them up, and reduced the answer to shillings and pence.

"Take off your hat," the King said to the Hatter.

"It isn't mine," said the Hatter.

"*Stolen!*" the King exclaimed, turning to the jury, who instantly made a memorandum of the fact.

"I keep them to sell," the Hatter added as an explanation: "I've none of my own. I'm a hatter."

Here the Queen put on her spectacles, and began staring hard at the Hatter, who turned pale and fidgeted.

"Give your evidence," said the King; "and don't be nervous, or I'll have you executed on the spot."

This did not seem to encourage the witness at all: he kept shifting from one foot to the other, looking uneasily at the Queen, and in his confusion he bit a large piece out of his teacup instead of the bread-and-butter.

Just at this moment Alice felt a very curious sensation, which puzzled her a good deal until she made out what it was: she was beginning to grow larger again, and she thought at first she would get up and leave the court; but on second thoughts she decided to remain where she was as long as there was room for her.

"I wish you wouldn't squeeze so," said the Dormouse, who was sitting next to her. "I can hardly breathe."

"I can't help it," said Alice very meekly: "I'm growing."

"You've no right to grow *here*," said the Dormouse.

"Don't talk nonsense," said Alice more boldly: "you know you're growing too."

"Yes, but *I* grow at a reasonable pace," said the Dormouse: "not in that ridiculous fashion." And he got up very sulkily and crossed over to the other side of the court.

All this time the Queen had never left off staring at the Hatter, and, just as the Dormouse crossed the court, she said, to one of the officers of the court, "Bring me the list of the singers in the last concert!" on which the wretched Hatter trembled so, that he shook off both his shoes.

"Give your evidence," the King repeated angrily, "or I'll have you executed, whether you're nervous or not."

"I'm a poor man, your Majesty," the Hatter began, in a trembling voice, "and I hadn't begun my tea—not above a week or so—and what with the bread-and-butter getting so thin—and the twinkling of the tea—"

"The twinkling of the *what*?" said the King.

"It *began* with the tea," the Hatter replied.

"Of course twinkling *begins* with a T!" said the King sharply. "Do you take me for a dunce? Go on!"

"I'm a poor man," the Hatter went on, "and most things twinkled after that—only the March Hare said—"

"I didn't!" the March Hare interrupted in a great hurry.

"You did!" said the Hatter.

"I deny it!" said the March Hare.

"He denies it," said the King: "leave out that part."

"Well, at any rate, the Dormouse said—" the Hatter went on, looking anxiously round to see if he would deny it too; but the Dormouse denied nothing, being fast asleep.

"After that," continued the Hatter, "I cut some more bread-and-butter—"

"But what did the Dormouse say?" one of the jury asked.

"That I can't remember," said the Hatter.

"You *must* remember," remarked the King, "or I'll have you executed."

The miserable Hatter dropped his teacup and bread-and-butter, and went down on one knee. "I'm a poor man, your Majesty," he began.

"You're a *very* poor *speaker*," said the King.

Here one of the guinea-pigs cheered, and was immediately suppressed by the officers of the court. (As that is rather a hard word, I will just explain to you how it was done. They had a large canvas bag, which tied up at the mouth with strings: into this they slipped the guinea-pig, head first, and then sat upon it.)

"I'm glad I've seen that done," thought Alice. "I've so often read in the newspapers, at the end of trials, 'There was some attempt at applause, which was immediately suppressed by the officers of the court,' and I never understood what it meant till now."

"If that's all you know about it, you may stand down," continued the King.

"I can't go no lower," said the Hatter: "I'm on the floor, as it is."

"Then you may *sit* down," the King replied.

Here the other guinea-pig cheered, and was suppressed.

"Come, that finishes the guinea-pigs!" thought Alice. "Now we shall get on better."

"I'd rather finish my tea," said the Hatter, with an anxious look at the Queen, who was reading the list of singers.

"You may go," said the King, and the Hatter hurriedly left the court, without even waiting to put his shoes on.

"—and just take his head off outside," the Queen added to one of the officers; but the Hatter was out of sight before the officer could get to the door.

"Call the next witness!" said the King.

The next witness was the Duchess's cook. She carried the pepper-box in her hand, and Alice guessed who it was, even before she got into the court, by the way the people near the door began sneezing all at once.

"Give your evidence," said the King.

"Shan't," said the cook.

The King looked anxiously at the White Rabbit, who said in a low voice, "Your Majesty must cross-examine *this* witness."

"Well, if I must, I must," the King said with a melancholy air, and, after folding his arms and frowning at the cook till his eyes were nearly out of sight, he said in a deep voice, "What are tarts made of?"

"Pepper, mostly," said the cook.

"Treacle," said a sleepy voice behind her.

"Collar that Dormouse," the Queen shrieked out. "Behead that Dormouse! Turn that Dormouse out of court! Suppress him! Pinch him! Off with his whiskers!"

For some minutes the whole court was in confusion, getting the Dormouse turned out, and, by the time they had settled down again, the cook had disappeared.

"Never mind!" said the King, with an air of great relief. "Call the next witness." And he added in an undertone to the Queen, "Really, my dear, *you* must cross-examine the next witness. It quite makes my forehead ache!"

Alice watched the White Rabbit as he fumbled over the list, feeling very curious to see what the next witness would be like, "—for they haven't got much evidence *yet*," she said to herself. Imagine her surprise, when the White Rabbit read out, at the top of his shrill little voice, the name "Alice!"

CHAPTER 12

Alice's Evidence

"**H**ere!" cried Alice, quite forgetting in the flurry of the moment how large
she had grown in the last few minutes, and she jumped up in such
a hurry that she tipped over the jury-box with the edge of her skirt,
upsetting all the jurymen on to the heads of the crowd below, and there they
lay sprawling about, reminding her very much of a globe of goldfish she had
accidentally upset the week before.

"Oh, I *beg* your pardon!" she exclaimed in a tone of great dismay, and began
picking them up again as quickly as she could, for the accident of the goldfish kept
running in her head, and she had a vague sort of idea that they must be collected
at once and put back into the jury-box, or they would die.

"The trial cannot proceed," said the King in a very grave voice, "until all the
jurymen are back in their proper places—*all*," he repeated with great emphasis,
looking hard at Alice as he said so.

Alice looked at the jury-box, and saw that, in her haste, she had put the
Lizard in head downwards, and the poor little thing was waving its tail about in a
melancholy way, being quite unable to move. She soon got it out again, and put it
right; "not that it signifies much," she said to herself; "I should think it would be

quite as much use in the trial one way up as the other."

As soon as the jury had a little recovered from the shock of being upset, and their slates and pencils had been found and handed back to them, they set to work very diligently to write out a history of the accident, all except the Lizard, who seemed too much overcome to do anything but sit with its mouth open, gazing up into the roof of the court.

"What do you know about this business?" the King said to Alice.

"Nothing," said Alice.

"Nothing *whatever?*" persisted the King.

"Nothing whatever," said Alice.

"That's very important," the King said, turning to the jury. They were just beginning to write this down on their slates, when the White Rabbit interrupted: "*Un*important, your Majesty means, of course," he said in a very respectful tone, but frowning and making faces at him as he spoke.

"*Un*important, of course, I meant," the King hastily said, and went on to himself in an undertone, "important—unimportant— unimportant—important—" as if he were trying which word sounded best.

Some of the jury wrote it down "important," and some "unimportant." Alice could see this, as she was near enough to look over their slates; "but it doesn't matter a bit," she thought to herself.

At this moment the King, who had been for some time busily writing in his notebook, called out "Silence!" and read out from his book, "Rule Forty-two. *All persons more than a mile high to leave the court.*"

Everybody looked at Alice.

"*I'm* not a mile high," said Alice.

"You are," said the King.

"Nearly two miles high," added the Queen.

"Well, I shan't go, at any rate," said Alice; "besides, that's not a regular rule: you invented it just now."

"It's the oldest rule in the book," said the King.

"Then it ought to be Number One," said Alice.

The King turned pale, and shut his notebook hastily. "Consider your verdict," he said to the jury, in a low trembling voice.

"There's more evidence to come yet, please your Majesty," said the White Rabbit, jumping up in a great hurry: "this paper has just been picked up."

"What's in it?" said the Queen.

"I haven't opened it yet," said the White Rabbit; "but it seems to be a letter, written by the prisoner to—to somebody."

"It must have been that," said the King, "unless it was written to nobody, which isn't usual, you know."

"Who is it directed to?" said one of the jurymen.

"It isn't directed at all," said the White Rabbit: "in fact, there's nothing written on the *outside*." He unfolded the paper as he spoke, and added, "It isn't a letter, after all: it's a set of verses."

"Are they in the prisoner's handwriting?" asked another of the jurymen.

"No, they're not," said the White Rabbit, "and that's the queerest thing about it." (The jury all looked puzzled.)

"He must have imitated somebody else's hand," said the King. (The jury all brightened up again.)

"Please your Majesty," said the Knave, "I didn't write it, and they can't prove I did: there's no name signed at the end."

"If you didn't sign it," said the King, "that only makes the matter worse. You *must* have meant some mischief, or else you'd have signed your name like an honest man."

There was a general clapping of hands at this: it was the first really clever thing the King had said that day.

"That *proves* his guilt, of course" said the Queen: "so off with—"

"It doesn't prove anything of the sort!" said Alice. "Why, you don't even know what they're about!"

"Read them," said the King.

The White Rabbit put on his spectacles. "Where shall I begin, please your Majesty?" he asked.

"Begin at the beginning," the King said, very gravely, "and go on till you come to the end: then stop."

There was dead silence in the court, whilst the
White Rabbit read out these verses:

"They told me you had been to her,
  And mentioned me to him:
She gave me a good character,
  But said I could not swim.

He sent them word I had not gone
  (We know it to be true):
If she should push the matter on,
  What would become of you?

I gave her one, they gave him two,
  You gave us three or more;
They all returned from him to you,
  Though they were mine before.

If I or she should chance to be
  Involved in this affair,
He trusts to you to set them free,
  Exactly as we were.

My notion was that you had been
  (Before she had this fit)
An obstacle that came between
  Him, and ourselves, and it.

Don't let him know she liked them best,
  For this must ever be
A secret, kept from all the rest,
  Between yourself and me."

"That's the most important piece of evidence we've heard yet," said the King, rubbing his hands; "so now let the jury—"

"If any one of them can explain it," said Alice (she had grown so large in the last few minutes that she wasn't a bit afraid of interrupting him), "I'll give him sixpence. *I* don't believe there's an atom of meaning in it."

The jury all wrote down on their slates, "*She* doesn't believe there's an atom of meaning in it," but none of them attempted to explain the paper.

"If there's no meaning in it," said the King, "that saves a world of trouble, you know, as we needn't try to find any. And yet I don't know," he went on, spreading out the verses on his knee, and looking at them with one eye; "I seem to see some meaning in them, after all. '—*Said I could not swim*—' you can't swim, can you?" he added, turning to the Knave.

The Knave shook his head sadly. "Do I look like it?" he said. (Which he certainly did *not*, being made entirely of cardboard.)

"All right, so far," said the King, and he went on muttering over the verses to himself: "'*We know it to be true*—' that's the jury, of course—'*If she should push the matter on*'—that must be the Queen—'*What would be come of you?*'—What, indeed!—'*I gave her one, they gave him two*—' why, that must be what he did with the tarts, you know—"

"But it goes on '*they all returned from him to you*,'" said Alice.

"Why, there they are!" said the King triumphantly, pointing to the tarts on the table. "Nothing can be clearer than *that*. Then again—'*before she had this fit*—' you never had fits, my dear, I think?" he said to the Queen.

"Never!" said the Queen, furiously, throwing an inkstand at the Lizard as she spoke. (The unfortunate little Bill had left off writing on his slate with one finger, as he found it made no mark; but he now hastily began again, using the ink, that was trickling down his face, as long as it lasted.)

"Then the words don't *fit* you," said the King, looking round the court with a smile. There was a dead silence.

"It's a pun!" the King added in an angry tone, and everybody laughed, "Let the jury consider their verdict," the King said, for about the twentieth time that day.

"No, no!" said the Queen. "Sentence first—verdict afterwards."

"Stuff and nonsense!" said Alice loudly. "The idea of having the sentence first!"

"Hold your tongue!" said the Queen, turning purple.

"I won't!" said Alice.

"Off with her head!" the Queen shouted at the top of her voice. Nobody moved.

"Who cares for *you*?" said Alice (she had grown to her full size by this time). "You're nothing but a pack of cards!"

At this the whole pack rose up into the air, and came flying down upon her; she gave a little scream, half of fright and half of anger, and tried to beat them off, and found herself lying on the bank, with her head in the lap of her sister, who was gently brushing away some dead leaves that had fluttered down from the trees upon her face.

"Wake up, Alice dear!" said her sister. "Why, what a long sleep you've had!"

"Oh, I've had such a curious dream!" said Alice. And she told her sister, as well as she could remember them, all these strange Adventures of hers that you have just been reading about; and when she had finished, her sister kissed her, and said, "It *was* a curious dream, dear, certainly; but now run in to your tea: it's getting late." So Alice got up and ran off, thinking while she ran, as well she might, what a wonderful dream it had been.

But her sister sat still just as she left her, leaning her head on her hand, watching the setting sun, and thinking of little Alice and all her wonderful Adventures, till she too began dreaming after a fashion, and this was her dream:—

First, she dreamed of little Alice herself: and once again the tiny hands were clasped upon her knee, and the bright eager eyes were looking up into hers—she could hear the very tones of her voice, and see that queer little toss of her head to keep back the wandering hair that *would* always get into her eyes—and still as she listened, or seemed to listen, the whole place around her became alive with the strange creatures of her little sister's dream.

The long grass rustled at her feet as the White Rabbit hurried by—the frightened Mouse splashed his way through the neighbouring pool—she could hear the rattle of the teacups

as the March Hare and his friends shared their never-ending meal, and the shrill voice of the Queen ordering off her unfortunate guests to execution—once more the pig-baby was sneezing on the Duchess's knee, while plates and dishes crashed around it—once more the shriek of the Gryphon, the squeaking of the Lizard's slate-pencil, and the choking of the suppressed guinea-pigs, filled the air, mixed up with the distant sobs of the miserable Mock Turtle.

So she sat on, with closed eyes, and half believed herself in Wonderland, though she knew she had but to open them again, and all would change to dull reality—the grass would be only rustling in the wind, and the pool rippling to the waving of the reeds—the rattling teacups would change to tinkling sheep-bells, and the Queen's shrill cries to the voice of the shepherd boy—and the sneeze of the baby, the shriek of the Gryphon, and all thy other queer noises, would change (she knew) to the confused clamour of the busy farm-yard—while the lowing of the cattle in the distance would take the place of the Mock Turtle's heavy sobs.

Lastly, she pictured to herself how this same little sister of hers would, in the after-time, be herself a grown woman; and how she would keep, through all her riper years, the simple and loving heart of her childhood; and how she would gather about her other little children, and make *their* eyes bright and eager with many a strange tale, perhaps even with the dream of Wonderland of long ago; and how she would feel with all their simple sorrows, and find a pleasure in all their simple joys, remembering her own child-life, and the happy summer days.

The End

Index

Page numbers in *italics* refer to illustrations.

Edited by: Theresa Best
Illustrations: Pierre A. Lamielle
Food photography: Julie Van Rosendaal
Typesetting by: Michelle Furbacher

Printed in Canada

**Library and Archives Canada Cataloguing
in Publication**
Van Rosendaal, Julie, 1970-
    Alice eats : a wonderland cookbook / Julie Van
Rosendaal.

Includes index.
ISBN 978-1-77050-191-1

    1. Cooking. 2. Cooking in literature. 3. Cookbooks.
I. Carroll, Lewis, 1832-1898. Alice's adventures in
Wonderland.
II. Title.

TX652.V36 2013   641.5   C2013-900951-5

The publisher acknowledges the financial support of
the Government of Canada through the Canada Book
Fund (CBF) and the Province of British Columbia
through the Book Publishing Tax Credit.

13 14 15 16 17   5 4 3 2